Discover everyday heroes and step into amazing new worlds with original series stories from endlessly imaginative author Kari Kilgore.

Dreams coming true after years of hard work.
Hugh savors every long-anticipated moment.
But a friend in desperate need reaches out.

Walt loves a good snowstorm settling in.
And a chance to help people who need him.
Until a good kid goes missing at the worst time.

Returning home thrills Beth and her sweet dog Janie.
A chance to breathe and listen her heart's voice.
But a missed appointment sets Beth on edge.

Andre loves cat-sitting for his best friend Dana.
Enjoying the peace and quiet of the neighborhood.
Until he hears a sound too disturbing to ignore.

George knows his kids got a great start.
But he struggles to adjust to life without them.
Then a change he can't ignore bursts into his life.

The Changes Cascade

Near Future Forward (with Jason A. Adams)

Dispatches from the Galaxy: A Space Opera Novella Trio

Dangerous Days on a Pleasure Planet

Storms of Future Past:

Dreaming the Storm

Joining the Storm

Into the Storm

Fighting the Storm

Storms of the Heart

Storms of Future Past Omnibus

Voices Through Time:

Songs in the Mountain

Secrets in the Land

Sorrows in the Earth

Walking the Ghosts

The Odd Society:

Independent by Means of Magic

Protected by Means of Magic

Collections:

Fantastic Shorts: Volume 1

Fantastic Shorts: Volume 2

Fantastic Shorts: Volume 3

Escape into Romance

Stepping Out of Reality

Hacking Cybercrime

Investigations Beyond Belief

Passages in the Real World

Fantastic Side Trips

A Kaleidoscope of Cat Tales

A Tapestry of Holiday Tales

Aunties Among Us

Four-Legged Heroes

Anthologies *with Jason A. Adams*:

Partners in Romance

Shadows Mountain Deep

Uncommon Holidays

Partnership in Crime

KARI KILGORE

Facing Down Extraordinary

Spiral Publishing, Ltd.

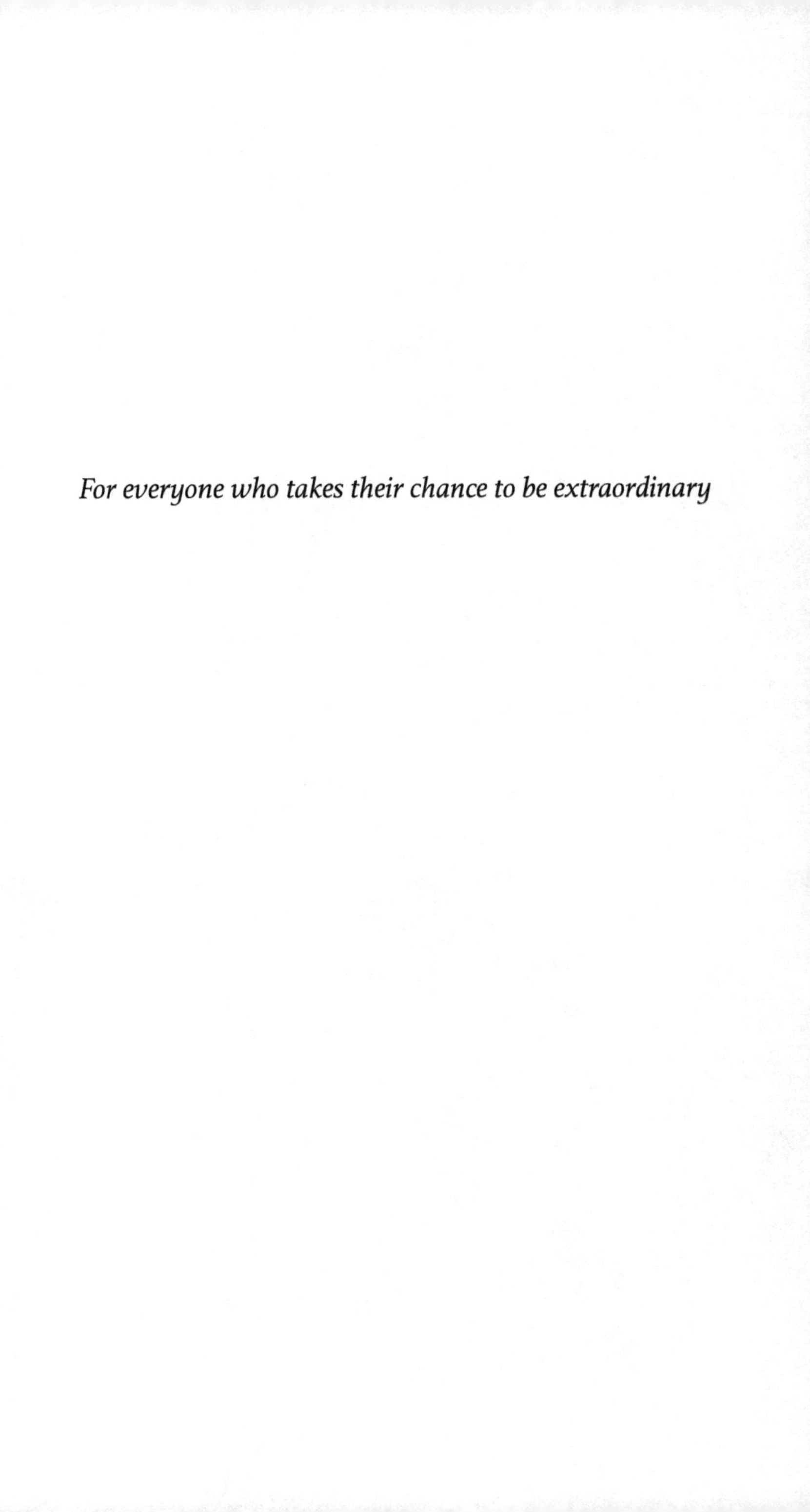

For everyone who takes their chance to be extraordinary

CONTENTS

SEIZING THE AMAZING DAY

Fictional stories, especially the ones that lend themselves to series, usually have heroic characters of one kind or another.

These aren't necessarily the folks flying around with capes or wielding magical weapons, though they certainly can be. Once you step away from the superhero genre, you'll often find heroes who don't see themselves that way.

They're often heroes to the people in their lives whether they realize it or not, and as readers, those are characteristics we love to see in ourselves.

Actions and traits we can honestly aspire to, as opposed to saving a city from a meteor strike or fighting an arch villain in a breathtaking aerial battle.

Sure, we need women and men who move mountains and perform superhuman feats to save the day. In storytelling and in life.

But we need ordinary, day-to-day heroes too. Possibly even more.

They're the folks who keep everything going. Train lines, our food supply, our computers. Helping others where they can even when that's *not* their job, but only because they have the chance to.

And because it's the right thing: a moment they simply can't walk away from without doing their best to make things better.

Sometimes when they're confused or over-whelmed or even scared to death, they do it anyway.

With that in mind, for the most part I approached my collection of hero stories by looking for those characters who keep everything going in the story world.

And for that, I turned to series and series charac-ters. Now they're front and center, and they have their chance to shine in stories that stand alone and apart from the series.

You don't have to be familiar with the series to read these stories, but I certainly hope you'll enjoy them enough to want to keep going.

Only one of these stories features a character who has other stories from her point of view. The rest are so-called side characters. Much like everyday heroes out here in the real world, these are the folks who help bring the story world to life.

Sometimes they're only onstage for a short time, but they're an important part of the tale. Sometimes they're so essential to the main character that the story wouldn't be the same without them, or it might not happen at all.

One of my favorite aspects of writing short stories within series is I get to follow fascinating side paths. The questions a main character has about their best friend or partner, or a past event that doesn't make it into the main narrative.

Many times the short story is simply me wondering where a side character came from. How they learned the vital skill or emotion or strength they bring to the main character. What made them who they are, and allowed them to enrich the story universe for me, the other characters, and hopefully for you, the readers.

In *A Soggy Brush with History*, we meet Beth Azen before she pairs up with Mark Hersch in my *Voices through Time* series. Beth's heroic nature—and her ability to catch whispers from an otherworldly source—is already front and center in this Appalachian tale.

We venture across the Atlantic to Scotland for *Decisions in a Dangerous Situation*, and delve into Hugh Fergusson's past. Hugh plays a crucial role in my contemporary fantasy novel *Hand Me Downs*, and I loved discovering one of the sources of his vast reserves of strength and confidence.

The Best Kind of Teacher returns to my native Appalachian Mountains, where we meet a younger version of Walt Colley. The tight-knit community in my series *Storms of Future Past* would struggle to survive without Walt and his steady encouragement and support. This prequel story reveals how far back his ties to magic go, and his willingness to share his magic.

In a twist that's absolutely perfect for the character, *Andre's Extra-Sensational Adventure* combines two different short story series. In one, Andre frequently teams up with cybercrime expert Dana Sanderson to solve near-future mysteries. In my *Terminalia* stories, people who never quite feel like they fit in are drawn to Atlanta, where they discover a growing connection to the multiverse. Since Andre is joyful, flamboyant, and in all ways *extra*, it's only fitting that he brings these two worlds together to make them that much more fabulous.

This collection draws to a close with a trip to Lightning Gap, Virginia, a lovely mountain town that's home to a peculiar sort of magic. The town itself hosts stories in more than one fantasy genre, and I learn more about how the magic lives and breathes with every visit. In *Sunny with a Chance of*

Happiness, George Edwards faces a tough transition for any parent. But as is always the case in Lightning Gap, the solution comes from an unexpected source.

I hope you enjoy getting to know these characters and reading these stories as much as I enjoyed writing them. Each is only a glimpse into a larger world with plenty to explore. You'll find doorways to them all at the back of the book.

For more Appalachian stories, head on over to www.KariKilgore.com/TalesfromAppalachia.

You'll discover more fantasy of many kinds at www.KariKilgore.com/Fantasy.

Check out all kinds of mysterious tales at www.KariKilgore.com/Mystery.

You can also visit www.KariKilgore.com to learn more about me and find other short stories, along with novellas, novels, and more collections.

If you want to keep up with what I'm doing next, get free stories, read exclusive content not available anywhere else, and see adorable pet photos, check out www.ConfidentialAdventureClub.com. Hope to see you there!

And last but certainly not least, thank you for your support of me and my writing. It means the world to me and keeps me coming back to tell the next tale.

Facing Down Extraordinary

KARI KILGORE

AUTHOR OF SONGS IN THE MOUNTAIN AND THE EARWORMS

A Soggy Brush with History

A Voices Through Time Story

For our sweet neighbor Myrtle

A SOGGY BRUSH
WITH HISTORY

As far as Beth Azen was concerned, nowhere was as lovely as the Appalachian Mountains in late summertime. Especially in and around her hometown of Hartstown, Virginia.

She drove along a tightly curved blacktop road, one narrow and remote enough that no one had ever bothered painting lines along the middle. The trees packed close alongside the road and the steep slopes it cut through were covered with lush, thick leaves in every shade of dark green.

The narrow verge along both sides was cut fairly short a few feet back, but beyond that weeds and brush grew wild and tall. A few towered above the rest, sporting the pale purple pyramid blossoms of Joe Pye weed or the zigzag yellow of goldenrod. Before too many days passed, another weed that could get past Beth's height of not quite six feet would join the party.

The striking violet blooms of ironweed would be the first signal that autumn was just around the corner. And just like every other flower that was already on the scene, all the moths and butterflies and honeybees would swarm to get ready for the long winter.

But for now, Beth drove with the front windows of her black Maxima open, taking in the warm, September afternoon air. The road twisted alongside a good-sized creek, and the sides were too steep and narrow to let her see much of the sky. But what she could glimpse overhead was a clear and deep summer blue.

Not too humid today, with the promise of rain later on in the air along with the sweet fragrance of all those flowers.

A series of quick inhaled breaths from just over her left shoulder let her know her hound dog Janie was enjoying the aromas as well. Enjoying them a heck of a lot better than Beth ever could too, with that big sensitive hound nose of hers going directly to a brain perfectly tuned for scenting the air.

Janie snorted out, blowing her warm, doggie-scented breath toward Beth's ear and cheek, before she sniffed in again.

Beth smiled and reached back to rub Janie's

head. Turned out both of them were happy to leave Nashville behind and get themselves back to Virginia. Nashville was a great city, of course, and they'd lived in a fantastic tree-lined neighborhood with plenty of places to walk and explore.

But nothing quite matched the peace and quiet—and the comfort—of being back home.

She'd normally wear a t-shirt and jeans on a day like this, partly because she was relieved to escape even the relaxed business-casual atmosphere of most of her clients and job locations back in the city. But Beth had recaptured a bit of her professional researcher and writer wardrobe today for a special occasion.

Dark gray khakis and a short-sleeved button-up shirt in rich burgundy seemed appropriate for interviewing her own favorite high school history teacher. She couldn't do much with her shoulder-length curly brown hair, but she did have it caught back with a headband that matched her shirt.

She'd even made a point of brushing Janie until her red coat shone once Ms. Sinnett asked her to please bring that sweet dog she could hear offering all kinds of opinions over the phone. Promises of a big, fenced-in yard to play in didn't mean Janie didn't need to look her best.

Beth slowed when the Maxima's GPS warned her the turn was up ahead on the right. The much smaller but well-maintained gravel road from what Ms. Sinnett told her.

After thirty years of teaching high school in Hartstown, retiring out to the old home place seemed like the logical course for someone who'd just reached a youthful and healthy not-quite-sixty.

Most importantly, Ms. Sinnett had been tickled to get Beth's call, and happy to give the interview for a new book project Beth had been kicking around in the back of her mind. Just the kind of distraction Beth needed from an unpleasant breakup a few months ago.

When the last tie that kept her anchored in Nashville had given way and freed her to head back to the mountains.

Janie *woofed* low as Beth turned onto a much narrower—and steeper—road than she expected. It was barely wider than her car, and it curved out of sight along a smaller creek. The trees grew so close overhead that the sun barely got through at all.

"You're right, Janie-girl. Looks like we're heading into a real adventure on this one. I should have made you wear your seatbelt."

The air temperature dropped immediately, and even the smells changed. Now Beth caught the damp, mossy scent of the creek, and organic odor of countless layers of leaves decaying along the hillsides. She rolled the back windows down a little now that she was barely going fifteen miles per hour, and Janie instantly jammed her nose against the opening and snuffled away.

Sure, Beth would have to wipe the nose prints off next time she vacuumed up bunches of red dog hairs from the backseat. And every bit was worth it for the canine sensory joy currently going on behind her.

The right side fell into a couple of scary drop-offs where the road was built as level as it could be, but mostly Beth drove about five feet above the water. So near she heard it splashing with runoff from heavy rains over the last week or so.

And everywhere enough sunlight broke through, the roadside was packed full of the towering, colorful weeds. Close enough that they swayed in the wind of her driving past, and brushed the side of her car a few times. She doubted anyone had bothered to trim much at all, or else the growth had gotten ahead of trimming schedule with so much rain. The raised section between the two shallow ruts in the road had been knocked back, but not much else. The stubbly growth in the middle was coated with pale gravel dust.

Beth laughed as the car's GPS informed her she would be navigating off-road up ahead. Not likely in her low-slung sedan. Sure enough, the digital blue line she was following disappeared while the road continued on, with the black-and-white-checkered flag sitting well past that.

She doubted anyone would bother updating the map for only a couple of houses anytime in the new future.

In a few spots, the road straightened out for a few hundred brightly lit feet, and somehow got even more narrow. In a couple of spots, Beth couldn't properly call it wide enough for her Maxima any more, much less for the big road boats she remembered Ms. Sinnett driving.

Nothing for it but to slow down, keep to the left, and keep going.

After what felt like an hour with the strange distortion of driving somewhere new—but the GPS insisted was just short of two miles—the trees and brush drew back on the left side. An adorable little white house sat perched in the clearing, surrounded by a neatly trimmed lawn with a chain-link fence all around.

Janie let out her regularly scheduled *woof* as Beth slowed again.

"Yep, there's your temporary playground, Janie. Let me see if I can figure out where to park."

The road curved out to the right before starting another sharp climb, but a graveled stub jutted out beside the little one-story house. Beth frowned at the empty parking area and glanced at her car's clock.

Eleven minutes to three, and three was exactly what she and Ms. Sinnett had agreed on. Beth remembered well how quickly her former teacher's mood could turn from lovable grump to downright mad when anyone was late for class.

She hadn't mentioned anything about going out, or about not having a car. Not that public transit was any kind of an option in such a rural area, even in town.

No, there were wide-set big-car-sized depressions in the gravel close to the house, and no weeds grew in that spot at all. Someone parked here regularly.

Beth parked on the far side, away from what had to be Ms. Sinnett's regular spot, and turned off the engine. She tapped the steering wheel, listening to the engine ping and tick to itself.

Several of the tidy house's windows were open, with cheery yellow curtains visible through the screens. A front porch with a set of sturdy concrete steps took up the front side, complete with a porch swing and several chairs, all cushioned in matching yellow fabric. The main entrance was on the side facing Beth, where another shady little porch waited at the end of a flower-lined sidewalk.

A little shed beyond that porch held stacks of perfectly split firewood, almost all of it in quarter-rounds for easy loading into a wood stove or fire-place. Several logs waited for their turn beside the shed. Beth envied the careful preparation and supply of heat already dried and ready to go. She'd been too busy moving into her own cozy little woodstove-equipped house on the edge of town to pay enough attention to cold weather on the horizon.

Ms. Sinnett and the honeybees were way ahead of her.

She couldn't hear any sounds besides the soft breeze and songbirds enjoying the day, but that didn't necessarily mean no one was home.

Even from here, the house *felt* empty.

Beth automatically reached over her shoulder at a long, dramatic hound dog sigh close to her ear.

"Well, I can't let you into the yard if no one's here. But we can get out and knock to make sure instead of sitting out here like stalkers."

Beth grabbed the bright red leash from the seat beside her, grinning as Janie poked her head over the middle console. Presenting her matching red collar in anticipation of a romp.

Ms. Sinnett said she kept the yard for various nieces, nephews, their kids, and their dogs rather than having any pets of her own, but Beth still grabbed hold of the leash first thing when she stepped out and opened the back door. Even a short ride in the car could result in an overly eager and remarkably strong pup.

Janie bounded out and vigorously shook from

her long red ears to the black tip of her tail, then held her nose up for a good long sniff. Beth slipped in a gentle reminder before any hound-in-a-new-place shenanigans could take hold.

"Heel, Janie. We're here on a polite visit, remember?"

She was answered with big brown pleading eyes, their outline of the canine version of black eyeliner making the effect even more dramatic. Then Janie sneezed and took her place at Beth's left side.

Those weeks of puppy training back in Nashville paid off *almost* every time.

As they walked the few steps to a back porch painted a proper and lovely shade of pale haint blue, Beth strained to hear anything from inside the house. Not a trace of a TV or radio, or anyone walking or moving around at all. A few pink chairs for hot-day relaxation in the shade sat beyond the screen door, along with what looked like boxes full of toys for kids and dogs alike.

Janie happily set about investigating the squeaky toy and stuffed animal stash.

Beth tapped on the strip of metal in the screen door. Still nothing from inside. The yellow curtain over the wooden inner door's glass never twitched.

She hated to walk away without trying harder, but a polite little girl inside scolded that she couldn't possibly try to open someone's door when they weren't home.

Answered immediately by Beth's thirty-five-year-old knowledge of older folks in her family.

Ms. Sinnett was hardly *older* older, but she still might be hurt or something like it. Unable to get to the phone or the door, and not quite able to hear Beth's knock.

She compromised by trying the screen door's handle, reasoning that she could knock on the wooden door with a bit more authority.

But the screen door was locked, which made no sense at all if anyone was actually home.

Beth knew what she'd see before she got out her smartphone, but she tried anyway, on the porch and again as she and Janie headed back out to the car.

Not a single bar of service.

She finally spotted the familiar small gray satellite dish perched on top of the woodshed. A sure sign of someone who only had one way to get internet, which she'd used several times over the last few days sending emails to Beth.

Including one around eleven that morning making sure everything was still on.

"Okay, Janie, let's stretch our legs and give her a few minutes. Maybe she got held up in town or something."

Even as Beth joined Janie on a quick trot in one

direction on the gravel road and then back, she knew that didn't make sense.

Ms. Sinnett had been so excited about this visit, sending notes a couple of times a day asking about what Beth might be interested in. She'd asked which of her several delicious cookie varieties Beth preferred (crispy ginger spice sounded best), and whether she'd like tea or coffee (coffee: always coffee).

They'd shared their frustration that a couple of members of the Boun County Historical Society were being oddly stingy with time and materials. She'd even suggested ideas for areas of the town's often-tragic history that Beth might want to concentrate on during the interview.

None of that added up to her just not being here.

By half past three, several more jogs, and lots and lots of nose-first investigations, Janie was panting and Beth sweaty and dusty enough to admit something must have gone wrong. Probably innocent like a forgotten family obligation or another appointment, unlikely as that sounded.

Hopefully nothing unpleasant or just plain awful.

She fetched Janie's stainless steel water bowl out of the back floorboard—a miniature of the one she drank out of at home—and filled it out of the gallon jug of water she kept for the same reason. While

Janie noisily slurped it all down, Beth sipped some of her own water and glanced back at the house.

Simplest thing in the world, really. Get in touch, make sure everything is okay, and reschedule. No one who'd worked with bunches of people on non-fiction books and articles and projects for more than ten years would get upset over one case of crossed scheduling wires.

Not if they wanted to stay in the same business and work with the same people, especially in a small town.

Beth considered driving on up the mountain to check in with the family at the end of the road, see if they'd heard anything. But Ms. Sinnett had mentioned how they were all either at work or school during the day, and while they were perfectly friendly and nice, she didn't mind the extra privacy one little bit.

It made more sense to head back into town where she could check her email, then call and leave a friendly voicemail.

She loaded a still-panting but happy Janie up and got back into the car to do just that.

But an uneasy shiver of something *wrong* rippled up and down Beth's spine as she started the engine and backed out.

By the time she got down to the blacktop again, that shiver had intensified into a case of not-at-all-subtle goosebumps running along her arms. She sat for a minute, left turn signal on, again drumming her fingertips on the steering wheel.

Still no cellular signal, and she *knew* she was missing something.

The day had darkened while she and Janie got overly familiar with a short stretch of the road in front of Ms. Sinnett's house, and a few fat raindrops splatted on the dusty windshield.

Beth looked in the rearview mirror, where the road behind her had taken on a near-nighttime gloom. Janie grunted and sat up, staring into Beth's eyes in the mirror.

"You're right, Janie-girl. We have to go back up there."

A quick turnaround in a nearby driveway had the Maxima pointed back up the steep road.

The thick canopy overhead blocked out some of the rain, but it was starting to come down in earnest by the time Beth got to the straight stretch right below Ms. Sinnett's house. She flipped on the wipers, sure to get the glass good and smeary with mud for at least a minute or two.

Then one of those smears on the right seemed to *flash...*

Electric red?

Beth let off the gas for a second and looked that way.

What she saw had her hitting the brakes as hard as she dared in one of the narrowest spots on a newly wet gravel road.

She'd thought that section was too close to the creek to have many of the towering weeds. But in her worry about keeping her own car far enough to the left, she'd missed how a big section of the weeds over there was flattened instead.

And some kind of light was indeed blinking down below it.

"Stay here," Beth said absently as she killed the engine again, cracked the back windows a tiny bit, and stepped out. As if Janie could possibly do anything but stay where she was.

Several drops of much-colder-than-expected rain landed on her head, but Beth hardly noticed. She walked carefully toward the creek.

Out of the car and really paying attention, she was close enough to see the road was more than narrow here.

Part of it had slumped off.

And the bright red light behind the weeds still flashed in a frantic pattern against the gloom.

"Hello?" Beth held her breath to try to hear above the noise of the rain hitting about a million leaves all around her.

"Beth?" a faint voice called. "Oh thank *goodness*!

Be careful, honey, the road bed might still be soft right there!"

Hand over her pounding heart, Beth took several steps forward, past the missing section.

Where she could finally see a big green Chevy sedan that had to be at least fifteen years old on its side, wedged tight in the middle of the steep sides of the creek.

Beth had to try twice to get enough breath to shout.

"Ms. Sinnett? Hang on, I'm coming!"

Beth scrambled down the bank, only about six feet at that point but soft from all the recent rain even before what felt like a new downpour got started. From this angle, she saw a car-sized gap in the roadbed, and big piles of reddish mud and bunches of white and gray mounded up along the side of the car.

The front windshield was shattered but intact, and covered with too much mud to see through. Beth didn't catch any scent of gasoline over the muddy smell of rushing water. She splashed ankle-deep in the cold creek, holding out a hand to make sure the radiator wasn't still hot.

It was almost as cold as the water.

She braced herself against the Chevy's hood and scooted forward between it and the creek's opposite bank, then scrambled up onto the side of the big car.

She couldn't tell if the passenger side window was broken out or rolled down like hers had been.

"I hear you out there, Beth, be *careful!*"

Beth crouched over the window and saw her former teacher inside, sitting at an awkward angle against the driver side door. Her sensible navy-blue blouse and pants were covered in red and brown muck, and streaks of it decorated her face and short silver hair.

"Are you okay?" Beth said, shifting back toward the hood so she could try and grab hold of the door handle. "How long have you been here?"

Ms. Sinnett shook head and smiled, but it was pained.

"I have to say I've been better. I don't think anything is broken, but I wrenched my back a good one when the car went over. Damn roadbed gave way right under me. That was... What time is it now, it *can't* be three o'clock already?"

Beth gave up on trying to lift the door from that angle and climbed across to the back door, shifting in the huge glops of mud. She was afraid it wasn't going to work. From the way the support pillars were twisted and crunched, the door might very well be jammed.

And she'd had too many experiences with a car parked sideways on a hill to think opening a big door with the car actually on its side would be easy.

"It's quarter to four," she said, straining against the door with no success. "I'm *so* sorry I missed you on the way in. I didn't see your brake lights flash until it got so cloudy. I can't get the door to move, is it locked?"

Ms. Sinnett laughed, then her face twisted in a grimace.

"It's not locked, I did that first thing when I thought I might be able to climb up there. Don't apologize, I just wish the blasted horn was working, might have helped. You don't mean to say I've been stuck in here for almost five *hours*? No wonder I'm so stiff I can barely move."

Thunder rumbled in the distance, and Janie answered with her usual volley of furious barks at the noise.

"Listen, we've got to get you out of there," Beth said. "The last thing you need is to get soaked by the rising creek in this storm, or have more of the bank slump down on your head."

"My backside is already soaked, and my right side was earlier. That's why I got myself out of the seatbelt and twisted around as much as I did. Driving with both windows open on a pretty day, of course. Best thing to do when you're about to splash down into a creek."

Beth stretched out flat across the car's side, reaching as far as she could inside. She couldn't quite reach Ms. Sinnett's shoulders, not across that wide interior.

Ms. Sinnett's hand was startlingly cold when she reached up and caught Beth's in a weak grasp.

Even if she could get both hands under Ms. Sinnett's shoulders, Beth was pretty sure she couldn't actually lift someone almost as tall as herself straight up that far.

"Can you stand?" she said. "Maybe push up and brace against your seat? I might be able to help pull you through."

Ms. Sinnett looked up and shook her head.

"I've been trying to, Beth. Even if I wasn't wedged in here with this big steering wheel, my back seizes up something awful. Not that this cold water running along my ass-end is helping much."

Beth blew out through her lips in frustration. The rain might have been blocked by the trees back where she'd parked, but out here under the break in the trees, her own ass-end was getting a good soaking.

Once again, the sensible voice demanded attention inside her whirling mind.

She should ask for Ms. Sinnett's house keys, then head back up to the house and call 911. Or even drive down to a neighbor's house instead if she had to. Then hand down some water and cover the window she was hovering over and block the rain from making it even more cold and wet inside the car.

Not that any of that would do a thing for the muddy creek water she could see building up through the driver's side window now. And that would only get worse with a thunderstorm that was promising to settle in and stay a while.

Not *drowning* worse, at least she didn't think so.

But bad enough that she couldn't just drive away.

"Okay, listen, I'm thinking I can help lift you out if I can get in there with you. Can you scoot forward so I can stand on the side of your seat? Or maybe I should just aim for the steering wheel."

Ms. Sinnett shook her head and frowned.

"Lord honey, if you're not careful we'll both end up trapped in here, and stay that way until one of my neighbors' kids comes roaring along in a couple of hours. Maybe you should just go up to the house and call the rescue squad instead."

Beth eyed the Chevy's interior, trying to gauge where she could push herself out if she actually got inside without landing right on top of Ms. Sinnett.

The steering wheel was doubtful, especially with mud-sloppy feet. The seats, maybe, but could she manage to push both of them out? Especially with Ms. Sinnett's back hurt in some unknown way?

Her next thought of grabbing a rock from the creek, or maybe some of the firewood from the house, to try to break out the windshield conjured up instant visions of knocking either herself or Ms. Sinnett in the skull with a badly aimed projectile.

Another boom of much-closer thunder and Janie's rapid-fire response made up Beth's mind.

The thought of her sweet dog trapped inside her own car—and with a teenaged driver possibly the first to come barreling along the now-muddy road—pushed the whole thing into too many risks.

She thumped her fist against the door and swore under her breath.

"I hate to say this like you wouldn't believe, but can you get to your house keys? Everything I can think of to do is seeming crazy enough inside my head that I'm afraid you're right."

Ms. Sinnett snorted and shook her head, then reached up to pull a set of keys Beth hadn't noticed out of the ignition.

"They're right here, attached to my car keys. This has been a good old tank for a lot of years, but it's nowhere near fancy enough to have a push-button starter."

She winced as she held the keys up, and Beth leaned through the window with both arms to make sure she had a firm grip.

The true nightmare scenario at this point would be dropping them into the swirling muck still gathering in the car, or right through the open window and into the rushing creek itself.

"Now listen," she said, grunting as she pushed herself back up against the rain-slicked metal. "I'm going to grab you a bottle of water, and set up my umbrella over this window before I go. I'll leave my car at your place so I won't block the tow truck or whatever else they send out, but I'll get back down here as fast as I can. I'm sorry I can't think of anything faster. Just hang on, okay?"

Ms. Sinnett raised one eyebrow and pursed her lips in an expression Beth remembered all too well from her school days.

She was in for a scolding, and through her guilt of having to leave another person in such a rotten situation, even for a few minutes, Beth knew she deserved to get fussed at.

"You're doing *plenty*, Beth, you hear me? If you hadn't come back—and yes, I know you left and came right back up here—I'd be sitting here for who knows how much longer. That and one of those poor kids might have skidded their car right in on top of me in this storm. Don't you *dare* feel guilty."

Beth nodded and smiled. Before she could say a word, Ms. Sinnett held up one muddy finger.

"One more thing before you go. Do me a favor and let your sweet dog out into the yard up there, would you? She can take herself right up on the porch and make herself comfortable out of all this rain. At least one of us should be warm and dry, right?"

"Right, and thank you. I'll get back as soon as I can."

In the end, the rescue squad and tow truck folks ended up knocking the windshield out themselves, then strapping Ms. Sinnett to a backboard to carry her out. Her back injury turned out to be a good, hard sprain rather than anything permanent.

Her much-loved old tank of a Chevy turned out to be the only thing that wouldn't recover with rest and time.

After a good night's sleep, and wearing her favorite jeans and a t-shirt rather than trying to scrub out her filthy nice clothes, Beth stopped by for a visit. Ms. Sinnett was staying with her sister in Hartstown for a few days to give her back a chance to recover.

And to let folks spoil her rotten, if her sister was telling the truth.

When Beth walked into the bright, cozy bedroom, one glance told her the sister hadn't fibbed even a tiny bit.

The white dresser, chest-of-drawers, and bedside tables were covered with potted plants, colorful get-well cards, and hand-written notes. A veritable forest of decorative balloons bobbed and swayed in the warm breeze from the open windows.

The spicy, sweet aroma of the freshly baked cookies tucked onto the table got all the attention of Beth's mouth and stomach.

In the middle of it all, Ms. Sinnett sat propped up in a little-girl-style canopy bed with fluffy pink blankets and pillows. She wore a matching cotton robe with pajamas covered in big yellow ducks peeking out underneath.

As soon as she saw Beth, she put down her book and grinned.

"Oh Beth, I'm *so* glad to see you! Do you have that sweet Janie with you?"

Beth sat in a white chair beside the bed, smiling at the frilly pink cushions tied onto the seat and back.

"Not today. I figured she'd want to snooze at home after all the excitement of yesterday. How are you feeling?"

Ms. Sinnett waved her hand as if she hadn't just been in a car accident barely twelve hours before.

"I'm fine, just covered up with people fussing over me. To tell you the truth, the doc gave me good enough drugs that I feel better than I have in years. Listen, you won't believe who stopped by this morning, and you *definitely* won't believe what she said.

Mrs. Betsy Sue Scarberry from down at the historical society, that's who."

Beth blinked, not sure if she should be excited or apprehensive. Mrs. Scarberry was the one cheerleading for not cooperating with Beth on her maybe-essay-growing-into-book history project.

"Well, Ms. Sinnett, if it's her, I'm not about to guess what she said."

Ms. Sinnett tilted her head to the side, and her scolding eyebrow darted up.

"You know, I've never understood exactly why fully grown people I just happened to have in my classroom a long time ago insist on being so darn formal all the time. I'll make you a deal. If you promise to at least try to call me Lucy, I'll tell you what Mrs. High and Mighty for No Good Reason told me."

Beth laughed before she could stop herself and held up one hand.

"Okay, I can't resist with bait that strong. When I slip up, just let me know and I'll try again. What did Mrs. Scarberry tell you, *Lucy*?"

"That's so much better," *Lucy* said with a single nod and a smile. "I think you'll feel like this is worth it. Despite all her silly and unreasonable objections, Mrs. Scarberry, who would very much *not* like to be called Betsy Sue, has decided to grant you full access to all the materials the historical society has. She figures she can get you in good with the other towns nearby, and probably in other counties, too. She knows with you being so good with computers and graphics and scanning and all, they can trust you to do the job right."

"Wow." Beth shook her head, hoping her grin didn't look too dopey, as if she were the one on the top-notch pain medication. "That's fantastic, thank you. I don't know if I'd ever be able to do anything with the other counties, but I sure do appreciate the trust."

This time Ms. Sinnett—*Lucy*—threw both hands up and rolled her eyes.

"Of *course* you'll do something with the other counties, Beth. I didn't get a chance to tell you this before my big creek adventure, but since you came back I've read all of the books you've worked on, and a bunch of your articles and essays, too. You're the very one we need to put together books of our history, right here. Hartstown and Boun County have had way more than their fair share of tragedy, sure, just like so many places out here in the coalfields have. But the best thing we can do about that now is make sure it's all recorded and written down. Before it all gets forgotten or twisted into nothing but rumors and fiction."

Beth opened her mouth to say no, then snapped it closed.

That was exactly what she'd been contemplating in the back of her mind, ever since she got settled in enough to slow down and think about what to do next.

The more she learned with her tentative investigations about that strange and colorful—and yes, deeply tragic—history, the more she *wanted* to put it together. Not just in another long-winded and dry book either.

She wanted to create something people would enjoy and be proud of, every bit as much as she would.

Beth met her former history teacher's excited gaze and smiled.

"That's exactly what I had in mind, Lucy. Between you and me, I know we'll come up with something amazing."

KARI KILGORE

Decisions in a Dangerous Situation

A Soul Travelers Story

For everyone who's afraid

and steps up anyway

CHAPTER 1

FOR MOST OF HIS LIFE, Hugh Fergusson believed moving house was one of the worst torments imaginable.

When his parents took the whole brood of them from one Glasgow neighborhood to another in the late 60s. When he moved himself to start university there in the early 70s. Even when he moved with his beloved wife Carolyn to Edinburgh at the end of that same decade.

The drudgery of realizing exactly how much rubbish he'd accumulated, packing it up, cleaning after himself, then reversing the whole process to move *in* filled him with dread.

So to be smiling as he stood in yet another new home, surrounded by a jagged mountain of boxes with more to come, and a sprawling garden outside that needed quite a bit of tidying, felt like a small miracle.

The early summer breeze coming through the open—and so far uncurtained—windows explained a huge part of his adjusted mood. Cool and crisp with recent rain, and fragrant from a wildly overgrown thicket of roses in red and white and yellow. The roses reminded him powerfully of a great sprawl in front of his mother-in-law Elizabeth's house in North Wales.

Lovely in their own way, much like she was. But prickly and quite capable of drawing blood if you weren't paying close attention, again much like Elizabeth.

Much like that land hours to the southwest, the air here carried not a trace of any sort of petrol stink from a nearby motorway.

No motorway sounds, either, not like he and Carolyn had slowly gotten used to over a decade in their otherwise charming Edinburgh flat. Here it was quiet enough that Hugh caught a chorus of birdsong to go along with the whisper of pine, rowan, and oak trees swaying in the garden.

The *garden*.

Their garden, his and Carolyn's, full of unruly grass and trees and flowers, and theirs to do with as they wished. Much like the unfortunate pale blue walls and dreadful brown carpets throughout the cozy two-bedroom house.

Close enough to the city so they could both drive in for work, and far enough to create an entirely new life for the two of them. Hopefully *three* of them at some point in the near future.

They wouldn't be sharing these walls with anyone else, or pretending to ignore whatever they heard going on through them.

Even faced with the rather filthy prospect of ripping up those carpets and the reek of fresh paint that would linger for days, Hugh grinned and picked up another box, this one actually meant to stay in the living room where he stood.

He deposited it with several others full of books, their stereo and LPs, and photos that would eventually bring the warmth and comfort of home to this empty space.

Right beside a gleaming black metal box that would bring the literal warmth in cold weather. He'd never lived anywhere with a woodstove before, and he barely knew his way around the rather intimidating axe that hung on the wall inside a sturdy woodshed behind the house.

The pale wooden handle was as long as Hugh's arm, age-darkened where hands would grip. The rough steel of the axe head itself flared out to a gleaming sharp edge that looked as if it would slice through the toughest wood with hardly any effort.

Or take a nasty bite out of a careless thumb or finger.

He was greatly looking forward to learning more about both the axe and the stove, hopefully without too many injuries along the way. And to years of nights curled up with Carolyn, in front of a fire he created and tended himself.

Though he hadn't started the messy work just yet, he was relieved to have his and Carolyn's clothing already stowed in their bedroom. Neither of them had anything arranged or organized, but they could get hold of clean things at the very least.

He already looked forward to shedding his dusty moving-day t-shirt and jeans, and scrubbing sweat and grime out of his getting-a-bit-shaggy brown hair. Once Carolyn got back from seeing to the last delivery, they'd both work for a while longer, then get ready for their first dinner prepared in their new home.

As if the thought conjured her out of the fragrant air, he heard a car door slam outside, then quick footsteps up the walkway. Footsteps he'd recognize in any situation, and that never failed to gladden his heart.

Carolyn opened the heavy, rough-cut oak door before Hugh could get to it.

As small and compact as he was tall and broad-shouldered, with dark brown eyes to contrast with his blue, and the joyful balance to his own sometimes dark moods.

But this afternoon, a worried frown darkened *her* face, and she grabbed Hugh's hand and pulled him toward the only seating in the whole room so far. Carolyn perched on the horrid floral-patterned settee they'd inherited from his family without taking off her coat.

"What's happened?" Hugh said, trying very hard not to imagine something horrible before she even said a word.

"I stopped in to check the post, just to make sure the forwarding was arranged." A ghostly smile crossed her face as she pushed her damp brown curls over her shoulders. "A day's delay, but everything arrived. I had an urgent note from Lorna."

Hugh closed his eyes for a second, then reached for her other hand.

A good friend of both of theirs since their university days, Lorna had gotten away from a rotten marriage a few years ago. Not because she'd been able to escape the monster on her own, or because she'd relied on her family for help and support. Her friends had provided all the help and support they could, and she'd still struggled.

Not least because her now ex-husband truly was a well-hidden psychopath, in Hugh's opinion.

Lorna escaped because her ex made a string of worse-than-his-usual bad decisions and landed himself in prison.

"I hope all is well," Hugh said.

Carolyn shook her head and looked toward the towers of boxes. Her soft North Wales accent got stronger when she was angry, even compared to Hugh's broad Glaswegian.

"All *was* well until that bastard Stuart was let out early. She should have had two more years to depend on, but now he's a free man."

Of all the things Hugh had stopped himself from imagining, this hadn't made the list. He'd been as relieved as Carolyn when the police and courts decided to protect random strangers in bars from Stuart, even as they were disgusted the same authorities wouldn't act to protect Lorna.

"He hasn't gone round to bother her, has he?"

Carolyn turned back to him, eyebrows raised.

"Did you think he would have possibly gone anywhere else? Stuart's only signs of cleverness or creativity are all related to how he mistreats people. When he can get away with it, of course, and after he's spent enough time playing the role of the perfect gentleman first. I doubt it ever crossed his diseased mind to do anything else. Thank the gods Lorna was out of town that day."

"Where is she now?"

"Staying with her sister in Dalkeith. And before you ask, since you're probably assuming everyone will be thinking rationally, Lorna has already been in contact with the police. Who are *not* thinking rationally, because they won't do anything *for* her until Stuart does something *to* her. That family of hers is no better, as usual."

Hugh's heart and stomach sank, even though he was hardly surprised. He'd heard many of the conversations between Lorna and Carolyn, both before Stuart was finally put away and after. He wished he could dispute that lack of interest from the police, or the lack of support from Lorna's family.

She was caught in a dangerous trap of the small town she lived in and the even smaller minds she lived among.

"Stuart must know where her sister lives," Hugh said. "She's been in Dalkeith for years. Lorna can't stay there."

Carolyn squeezed his hands and let go, then scooted round until she sat sideways with one leg curled under her.

Moving so she could look him directly in the eyes.

Knowing *why* she did it didn't give Hugh any more of a chance of resisting her.

"You're thinking she should stay in a shelter instead," Hugh said, deliberately misunderstanding.

But hoping he was right.

"She could do. But only for a few days. Much of an arsehole as Stuart is, he'd surely manage to wait her out that long, unless he does something else to get himself picked up. I'm afraid the shelters wouldn't be all that hard to find."

Even as he badly wanted to put Carolyn off, a snarl of guilt worked its way through Hugh's heart and mind. He was certain he knew what she was thinking, and it did make an undeniable sort of sense.

Hardly anyone knew they'd moved, outside of their own families. And no one had been out for a visit yet. This house and the open land around it, away from Edinburgh and even the nearest small village, was a near-secret at the moment.

The loyal, good friend thing to do would be have Lorna stay with them, of course. Move her into the guest bedroom that they didn't yet need for a child, and couldn't possibly need for at least nine months by the rules of basic biology.

Not that they'd discussed the start date for that next project between them, not in concrete terms.

The problem with considering having Lorna stay

here to avoid her bully of an ex-husband was Hugh didn't consider himself any sort of heroic figure. He was currently on two weeks' holiday from work as a computer programmer and designer, not anything remotely physical or brave.

The most he expected he could do in a dangerous situation was barricade the door and call for help.

And not one bit of that mattered with his wife staring at him with such confident expectation. She figured he'd agree with the rational course of action, as she said earlier.

He knew her well enough to know she was completely prepared to argue if need be, too.

"What is it you want to do, Carolyn?"

She let out an exasperated breath.

"Unless we can manage to smuggle her to Europe, or away to America, I think it makes sense for her to stay here. I expect Stuart will be after his old hooligans when he can't find her right away. If luck is with all of us, he'll fall into the same sort of trouble and get himself sent up for good."

"Have you spoken with Lorna about this?"

"Of course not." She leaned back and blinked. "I'd never do a thing like this without talking to you first. It's your house too."

Another little ripple of joy rose up at the thought —our house, and no one else's—but it was faint compared to how Hugh felt just a few short minutes before.

None of that changed the hope he saw in Carolyn's eyes.

"Then let's talk to her first and see how she feels," he said. "Now I feel like a pure coward saying this, but do you think Lorna will keep it to herself? Not let Stuart know where she is, or anyone who might tell him? I've never trusted him, and I don't want him here."

Hugh was a little ashamed of how relieved he was to see Carolyn look uncertain.

He wasn't the only one concerned. And she was taking the risk seriously.

"I don't think she'd say anything, or else she wouldn't have written to me. She has to know what he'd do if he found out. It wasn't easy for her, but now the last thing she wants is him back in her life."

"Now here's the second thing I don't feel good about saying. I don't want to risk you over this. And I don't want to look over my shoulder every time I come home, wondering whether he's found out and come round to settle the score at last."

Hugh waited out a terribly uncomfortable silence, watching Carolyn stare down at her hands and think it over.

"I don't want any of that either. I don't want the risk for you or for me." She looked into his eyes. "The other thing I don't want is to hear something awful has happened to her, and wonder what we could have done. Do you understand?"

Hugh rasped one hand across his stubbly cheek and nodded.

"I do understand. I haven't checked the phone but it's supposed to be connected today. Why don't you call her, love?"

Instead of smiling or jumping up right away, Carolyn closed her eyes for a moment.

"Thank you for listening, Hugh. And for being willing to consider this. I know I'm asking a lot. It's just... I have the strongest feeling she needs our help more than she's able to say."

Hugh pulled her into a hug, breathing in the scent of her hair mixed with the rain.

"It's all going to be all right, love," he said close to her ear. "Stuart isn't the sort who can help himself when it comes to acting out his true nature. You're right, he'll do something to get himself sent up soon enough."

He kept his worries about what that might be, and *where* it might be, to himself.

CHAPTER 2

Lorna arrived early the next afternoon, while Hugh was in the garden contemplating which of the overgrown and neglected areas to tackle first.

Grass? Roses? Rambling vines that entirely obscured the stone wall running alongside the road? Or perhaps the pile of too-thick logs beside the wood-shed that still needed splitting into usable firewood?

Every one of them reminded him how much his back, arms, and even his hands ached from all the box moving and unpacking the day before. And left him wondering how long it would take to get used to all the yardwork he and Carolyn had ahead of them after years in a no-maintenance flat.

Truly the sort of labor and adjustment they were both looking forward to, sore muscles or no.

The day was sunny and brisk, the brighter light reassuring him that the house itself was in reasonably good condition. The stone walls had been spared from the climbing-vine menace, and the dark gray of the slate roof sparkled in even and regular rows. He'd already had the squared-off chimney inspected, partly because he would have had no idea what to inspect for.

The road out of the nearest village was far enough away down their graveled driveway—gently curved with the contours of the land—to keep them from hearing traffic noise from inside the house. But out here Hugh couldn't help noticing the occasional car passing by.

And paying far more attention than he usually would.

His sensible and ordinary blue sedan waited alone in the rectangular parking spot. Carolyn should be back any time now in her green compact, which Hugh could barely wedge himself into.

She'd return with Lorna and at least a couple of weeks' of her clothing and things inside. Lorna had set out from Dalkeith on a bus, then switched to a hired car the rest of the way to the village.

Hugh told himself over and over again—every time a car drove past, really—that Lorna not driving herself was the smartest thing to do. Much less chance for Stuart to follow her, assuming he was desperate enough to even make the attempt.

He hadn't bothered her at her sister's house before she left. He'd never even shown his untrustworthy face.

Hugh had just finished stacking up the piles of logs in a more-or-less orderly fashion, grateful Carolyn couldn't hear his various grunts and groans as he did so, when he heard a car slow, then turn onto the gravel. He stretched with his hands pressed against the small of his back before walking out to meet Carolyn's little green car.

Even before the two of them got out, Hugh saw how much better Lorna looked than the last time he'd seen her. A habit she'd started once Stuart wasn't around to keep her too pale, too thin, and too exhausted.

She stood a bit taller than Carolyn, with her fine blonde hair loose in the breeze. She wore a red jacket against the chill, but it didn't hide the feminine curves that had gradually replaced a painfully boyish body that never suited her.

Lorna's green eyes were clear, but so was the tension in her face when Hugh reached them.

"I'm sick to hear about Stuart," he said, then he leaned in and kissed her cheek. "And it's lovely to see *you*, Lorna. Welcome."

Lorna let out a harsh breath on the way to catching him in a tight hug.

"Thank you," she whispered before she stepped back. "Thank you both for letting me stay. I promise to find somewhere else as soon as I possibly can."

Hugh gathered two suitcases from the back of the car, relieved they were fairly small even as the thought made him guilty. Too small for her to be planning a long stay.

"What you need is a holiday to start with," he said. "And no worries about rushing yourself out the door. If you're better at gardening than we are and you feel up to it, you'll be the one doing *us* a favor."

"I'm hardly an expert," Lorna said, surveying the wild landscape with her hands on her hips. "But between the three of us we can at least reclaim at bit of lost territory without doing too much damage."

He followed the two women, returning the smile Carolyn flashed over her shoulder.

He couldn't help looking over his own shoulder, though, at the sound of two cars passing by close together in the same direction, away from the village. Too far off to see who drove, or even what the cars looked like.

Not all that remarkable, even as remote as they were. Nothing he'd bother mentioning to Carolyn or Lorna.

Hugh knew he wouldn't forget the way the hair on his arms and the back of his neck stood to attention.

A decidedly odd response to what he worked very hard to convince himself was nothing at all.

CHAPTER 3

Lorna was as good as her word, heading out to work on the riotous roses as quickly as she could change clothes.

She reasoned they could at least get them tied back and propped up away from the ground and out of the damp. That way when someone who *did* know how to properly tend them arrived, it would be quick work. Neither Hugh nor Carolyn could argue with that logic. They both knew the elaborate supports of the roses back in Wales, built up over years of careful but not overly fussy tending.

By the time the light failed them, Hugh, Lorna, and Carolyn were covered in a variety of scratches and thoroughly rose-scented. And the bushes looked top-heavy but far more respectable.

Hugh didn't feel any more of those warning twinges the whole time they worked outside. Clearly he'd been overreacting to their unexpected guest's arrival. He did his best to convince himself the calm didn't mean trouble would only wait until dark, or at least until the three of them went inside.

When they let their guard down.

The most important thing was making Lorna feel welcome, challenging as that might be in a still-disorganized house.

Throwing his own paranoia into an already disrupted evening could only upset everyone, and for no good reason.

But it turned out Carolyn wasn't the only one who could see through his attempts to hide his feelings.

Lorna touched Hugh's shoulder as he gathered up the few garden tools they had to take around back to the shed. Not much more than a couple of hammers, bits of old lumber, a ball of twine, and a hacksaw, but they got the job done.

"You're sweet to worry over me, Hugh. But don't let Stuart get too much inside your head. He did that to me for years, and nothing good ever came of it. I didn't catch on to how much he twisted my brain until I was away from him."

"I can't say I don't see the difference in you," Hugh said. "And I'm glad of it. You're sweet to worry about me as well, but I won't rest easy until Stuart's no longer a threat to any of us."

Lorna shrugged and smiled, then walked off toward the house. Carolyn, carrying the twine and a few scraps of wood they hadn't needed for the roses, stopped beside Hugh. A few shiny green leaves and a couple of stray red petals had caught in her hair, and a shallow scratch decorated one cheek.

"She's doing well, I think," she said. "Incensed at the courts for letting him go early, and certainly without warning her. More disgusted with the police than angry at this point. Her family isn't worth mentioning. Are you feeling all right about all this?"

Hugh took her armful despite the way his own arms fairly trembled with overuse, then kissed her unwounded cheek.

"I'll feel better once Stuart's seen to one way or another, to be honest. It's good to have a place to bring a friend who needs us, you know?"

Carolyn stepped toward him, and he met her in a real kiss.

"I do know. We'll get started on dinner since we're all ravenous."

Hugh continued around the house, listening to Carolyn and Lorna chatting through the open windows. His formerly quiet stomach clamored for food now that someone had mentioned it, loud enough to hear even over his feet brushing through the tall grass.

So strange, after all the noise in the city, the way his ears seemed to strain for more input, catching every last bit of sound. The trouble with that was how *noisy* everything back in Edinburgh would sound after days spent here in paradise.

He paused just outside the rough wooden planks of the shed, struck by the low roar of a car out along the road when he hadn't heard one for a good long while.

A car that slowed rather than speeding along.

Then Hugh caught the crunch of gravel under tires.

Sudden silence from inside the house let him know Carolyn and Lorna heard it too.

"No, you don't need to go out there," Carolyn said beside the kitchen window, clearly upset and loud enough for her words to carry. "Let me call the—"

"What for? If it *is* him, you think the police will do a damn thing out here, any more than they did before?"

Hugh stepped into the shed, putting everything down as quietly as he could. Only a faint wash of light remained in the deepening blue of the sky, but he could see well enough to grab what he needed.

The thud of a car door in front of the house set his heart racing.

If that was Stuart—and Hugh couldn't imagine anyone else calling at this hour—he'd surely broken his parole license in driving all the way out here. But that parole and the sentence it freed him from had been based on the nonsense he got into with his hooligan friends.

Not the threat he'd been to his own wife.

Lorna might be right about struggling to get help from the police.

Hugh got a better grip on the axe handle, textured like grit against his palms, wishing his arms weren't as shaky from work as his hands were from nerves now.

He walked slowly toward the front of the house, listening for the faintest sounds.

At the deceptively polite knock on the front door, Hugh jumped and caught his breath. He waited, fighting to keep himself quiet and still.

The house was silent enough that it may as well have been empty.

Another knock.

"Lorna, I know you're here," a voice called. "A child could have followed you."

Calm and confident, without the slightest trace of anger or impatience.

Stuart, come to fetch his wayward wife back home.

With no expectation that anyone would dare interfere.

Hugh stepped carefully, trying his best to stay quiet against the grass.

"We should talk, don't you think?" Stuart said, every word giving Hugh more certainty that he hadn't moved away from the door. "We've been apart so long."

"Not long *enough*," Lorna spat, her voice angry and strong. "You're not part of my life any more, Stuart. No one wants you here."

And now Stuart would know exactly where she was inside the house.

Exactly where Carolyn was, too.

"I'm not going to force you to do anything you don't choose to," Stuart said. "You can't believe I was kept away from you so long without learning what I've done wrong?"

"I don't care what you've learned!" Lorna was now on the opposite side of the house, but Stuart might not be able to tell that. "You're not welcome here or anywhere else near me. Now *go!*"

He also wouldn't know how the inside of the house was laid out. Lingering boxes in the floor or not, that gave Hugh, Carolyn, and even Lorna a big advantage.

Hugh reached the corner, right before he'd be visible from the front door, leaning into the cold, rough stone of the house with one shoulder. The third vehicle behind his own was outlined in the fading light.

Stuart had parked sideways in an obvious move to block the entire driveway.

As usual, once you learned how to pay attention, his veneer of civility and appearance of concern was barely molecule-thin.

The monster underneath always broke through.

Hugh had just raised the axe in his sweating hands—with sincere doubts that he'd manage to do anything useful with it—when the glare of the newly installed light over the front door shattered his night vision.

By the time he blinked and looked back, he saw exactly what he dreaded and still knew he would.

Carolyn stood outside their closed front door, temporarily taller than Stuart, who'd stepped backward off the two stone steps. Arms crossed across her chest, chin held high, as if she faced down a fussy child rather than a man who'd finally been convicted for some of his violent crimes.

"You need to go, Stuart," she said. "You're *not* welcome, and I very much doubt your parole board would approve of you being here."

Stuart looked as if not a day had passed despite his time in prison. Same neat haircut and clean-shaven face. Same dark, pressed trousers and tidy sport jacket, as if he were on his way to an appointment or home from work.

Anyone who didn't know him would assume he was perfectly respectable and normal.

When he spoke, his voice was more like the blade of an ice-cold knife than anything resembling normal.

"Step aside, Carolyn. This doesn't concern you."

Hugh's feet carried him forward before his mind could make the decision, and his thundering heart kept him going.

"It concerns *me*, Stuart," he said, holding the axe low at his right side. "You've been told twice that you're not welcome here. You don't want me to explain it to you a third time."

Stuart grinned, dropping all pretense of the loving former husband eager for a reunion with his beloved estranged wife.

Now his eyes were as reptilian and cold as his voice.

"Finally decided to show yourself instead of letting the women keep you safe? I didn't come out here for you or your little wife, Hugh. Lorna is the only thing I'm concerned with, and I'll be taking what's mine. Unless you actually expect to do something with that pretty axe of yours."

Lorna shouted from inside before Hugh could answer.

"The police are coming, Stuart! You'll find yourself back inside no matter what, and it's what you deserve. Go on before you make it worse for yourself."

Hugh walked slowly forward, intent on getting himself between Stuart and Carolyn. Every other consideration, including his own physical safety, paled beside that.

Stuart winked at him and lunged toward Carolyn, lighting fast.

He dragged her from the steps, one arm round her waist, the other round her neck with a hand covering her screaming mouth. He lifted her off the ground, never seeming to feel her fists or heels crashing into his own body.

"No matter what, eh?" Stuart said, raising his voice above Carolyn's. "So I might as well enjoy myself while I'm here?"

Hugh closed the distance, raising the axe without thinking. His heart still pounded and every muscle sang out with tension, but his thinking had gone clear and steady.

"Ask yourself this, Stuart. Do you want to go back to prison with your body intact and whole, pathetic as that prospect might be? Or are you happy to return missing as many parts as I can hack off?"

Stuart twisted sideways, turning Carolyn and her fighting arms and legs toward Hugh.

Carolyn's furious gaze met Hugh's just as her jaw flexed under Stuart's fingers.

His lips drew back from his own teeth as Carolyn's sank into his flesh.

Stuart roared but he didn't let her go.

"Once more and I'll snap your pretty little neck! Or bash your skull against this bloody *house* for you, and your weakling of a husband will get to watch."

Hugh lunged to one side, then the other, but Stuart turned too fast.

Keeping Carolyn between them.

He couldn't catch a way through that didn't involve more risk than he was willing to take.

Until the heavy oak door opened and a screaming blur shot through.

Lorna crashed into Stuart's side hard enough to knock him staggering to the ground, breaking his grip on Carolyn.

Both women rolled free while Stuart flailed after them.

For the briefest instant—and the longest of Hugh's life—he saw the sharp blade of the axe slicing through Stuart's chest in excruciating, gory detail.

Through the legs Carolyn had kicked.

The arms he'd grabbed her with.

Leaving his chest with a gaping chasm where a heart should have been.

Destroying the diseased thing inside his skull.

He shifted his grip at the last second instead and crashed the flat side of the blade against Stuart's jaw.

Dropping him to the grass and leaving him to the tender mercies of his former wife.

Hugh let the axe slip from his hands and crouched beside Carolyn, ignoring the screams and thuds and Lorna took her long-awaited revenge.

"Come on, let's get you away," he said, slipping one arm under her shoulders. "Are you hurt?"

For the first time since Hugh had first caught sight of Carolyn her all those years ago at university in Glasgow, her smile made him queasy.

Stuart's blood lingered on her lips and teeth.

"I'm not hurt, but I wish I'd managed to do more than bite him. Are *you* hurt? You're shaking like a leaf."

Hugh stood with her, walking them a few steps away from Stuart's crumpled form.

And from Lorna, sitting back on her heels and quiet beside him.

"I'm fine, or at least uninjured. Did one of you really call the police?"

All the anger deserted Carolyn in that instant, and she wiped blood away from her mouth with a trembling hand. She finally looked as frightened as Hugh felt rather than ready to take Stuart apart without need of such crude tools as an axe.

"I don't know. I hope so."

She crossed to Lorna and knelt, keeping her distance from Stuart.

At one glance, Hugh knew Stuart wouldn't be bothering them or anyone else anytime soon.

Lorna's efforts had rolled him over, leaving the reddened swelling of Hugh's handiwork vivid in the harsh light. Several scuffed footprints against Stuart's carefully ordinary trousers and jacket told the tale.

His chest still rose and fell.

Hugh wasn't sure how he felt about that yet.

He knelt by Lorna's other side.

"...so sorry," she said, her voice rough. "I never should have come here and put you two in his path. I'll leave when the police are...are finished with him."

Carolyn already held both of Lorna's hands, so Hugh leaned close enough to put his arm around her shoulders.

"We *offered*, remember?" he said. "Stuart brought all of this on himself with the way he treated you and everyone else."

Carolyn looked at him over Lorna's bowed head, her eyes warm and relieved.

"He certainly did bring it on himself. And our offer still stands. You can stay here and get your wits about you, Lorna. Decide what you want to do next. Without the threat of Stuart hanging over your head."

Lorna took a deep breath and sat back, just as the

rapid rise and fall of police sirens cut through the quiet night. She glanced at Stuart, then turned a faint smile toward Hugh.

"We'll see what the next few hours bring, besides a meal we all very much need. But will you answer one question for me? The truth, now."

He nodded, hoping he'd be able to do that one small thing.

"Did you mean to hit him with the blunt side of the axe? Or did you simply miss?"

Hugh started to say of course he'd meant to, but he hesitated.

Checking inside to make sure that was a truthful answer.

"I wanted to hit him with the sharp side," he said, looking into Lorna's eyes, then Carolyn's. "I admit I considered it. But I decided not to at the last second. All right?"

Lorna studied him for a few seconds while the sirens drew closer, then nodded.

"I believe you did decide not to. I'm not sure I would have done the same. I think… I think I'm glad it didn't come to that."

The three of them got to their feet, and Lorna walked toward the road.

Waiting to meet the police, who would surely listen to her at long last.

Carolyn stepped into Hugh's arms, and he finally dared believe all could again be right with the world.

"All right with you as well?" he whispered close to her ear.

She squeezed him tight and leaned back to look into his eyes.

"As long as you're here, it is," she said. "As long as we're together."

KARI KILGORE

AUTHOR OF ODDS AND ENDINGS AND THE EARWORMS

The Best Kind of Teacher

A Storms of Future Past Story

For everyone who has the chance to help someone learn
and takes the time to do it right

THE BEST KIND
OF TEACHER

WALT COLLEY FIGURED he had to be shaving a year or two off his time in purgatory, but he wasn't so sure it was worth it.

The big, lazy snowflakes collecting on his faded purple Wolf Branch High School baseball cap weren't all that bad, even though they did get together and drop off past his eyes every few minutes. His big, rawboned hands felt the nip in the late afternoon air more than he liked, same as his toes in his scuffed brown leather steel-toed work boots.

He could tolerate the chill for a good while longer, especially in his sturdy blue work coveralls with a puffy brown jacket over top. The fresh, clean smell of a snowstorm heading in cheered Walt up pretty much no matter what else was going on.

The bright white drifting down hadn't gotten thick enough yet to obscure the red brick buildings of the smallish town of Wolf Branch stretching out all around him, but the sheltering bowl of the mountains had already disappeared, almost like they merged right in with the gray sky. That likely meant a long night of running snow plows and salt trucks in town, and possibly running tow trucks for folks who didn't pay attention to the weather warnings.

As far as Walt was concerned, as long as no one got themselves hurt with such foolishness, it was worth it for what promised to be a gorgeous sight of snow-covered trees come sunrise.

He didn't even mind the way nineteen-year-old Jimmy Adams talked about ten miles a minute, letting Walt and anyone else within shouting distance know he'd had something with plenty of garlic and onions for his lunch break before the snow got started.

That part *was* more or less hard to take, seeing as how Walt hadn't yet gotten to his own dinner bucket packed full of leftovers from his granny's big Sunday dinner feast the day before. After long hours working for the town—in the garage all day, getting ready for a heck of a lot more snow to settle in overnight—he sure could use a big mess of fried chicken, cornbread, green beans, and potatoes.

That kind of feast would keep him going right on through the night if need be.

Jimmy waved his arm again, without the slightest notion that he held an oversized crescent wrench in his hand. A wrench that wouldn't do a bit of good with any kind of modern automotive technology—like the big green Chevrolet truck he was having trouble with—unless you had a window that needed breaking for some ungodly reason.

Walt leaned back like he'd done every other time, then made a show of peering at the engine currently vexing Jimmy almost to the point of conniptions.

Walt kept his opinion of how that boy couldn't see what was right in front of his eyes if a spotlight big as the moon in the sky cranked up and shined right directly on the problem to himself.

He was bound and damned determined to let this goofy kid figure out the trouble on his own, not scold him or try to make him feel bad about all the things he didn't already know.

That, in Walt's long-considered opinion, was how you learned.

The engine was kind of a crusty mess, sure, just like most of the vehicles in the town's motor pool. They couldn't much escape that, driving up and down the Appalachian Mountain roads in any kind of weather, and when a good bit of the mileage they covered was still across mud and dusty gravel.

But like all the other vehicles in the town shop, Walt knew this truck was as well maintained as it could be. Or it *would* be, once Jimmy settled down enough to notice the simple trouble that had it running like a fifty-year-old junker instead of a perfectly good Chevy with less than fifty thousand miles on the odometer.

"Damndest thing I ever did see, Walt," Jimmy said for at least the tenth time. "I swear I got a tankful of bad gas last fill up, or maybe one of the filters has got itself full of all this salt and gunk all over the roads. All I know is it started chugging and wouldn't hardly pull coming up that hill headed into town."

Just then a big gob of snow dropped splat down off the *back* of Walt's baseball cap, right past his thick brown hair that he let grow out every winter for this very reason. Then down his shirt so it could melt and run down his back.

That was the worst thing about trying to help this sweet kid who didn't have the good sense to drive his ailing truck all the way around into the darkened hunk of the town garage instead of parking it on the street beside the town hall.

Sometimes Walt could just about smack himself upside the head for being too nice for anybody's good.

"And you say all the filters are new?" he said,

hunching up his shoulders and brushing the snow off his hat.

Jimmy finally gathered up enough awareness of his own hands to put the useless hunk of metal down in the big red toolbox he had balanced on the edge of the truck's open hood. He tipped his own smudged-up white ballcap back and scratched his thin blond hair.

"So you're saying that can't be it. Maybe I got a clogged fuel line, though, think that would make it run so bad?"

"You fill up at the town's pumps, like all the rest of us do with these work trucks?"

This time Jimmy turned and glanced toward the garage, where the pumps waited out of sight.

"Well yeah, like I always do. You're saying no one else is having this kind of trouble."

Walt shrugged and rubbed his big hands together to warm them up, or at least make it look like he was trying to.

Teaching or not, sometimes a hint or two wasn't a bad thing.

"Haven't heard of it from anyone else, no," Walt said. "Listen, you been out over any rough roads last couple of days? Rougher than usual, I guess I should say."

Jimmy laughed, but he rubbed his own hands

together and shoved them deep in the pockets of his dark-blue work pants.

"Sure thing, Walt. Had to go out along one of the old mine roads this morning. About jolted my teeth right out of my head." He stopped, staring at the engine, then at Walt. "Jolted something loose, *that's* what you're getting at. All the fluid levels are good, and no leaks on the ground."

Walt nodded, letting a half-smile break through.

"If those lines are good," Jimmy went on, "some other hose might have got knocked loose. Just got to figure out what's not getting through, right?"

"Want to start her up and we'll see what you can find?"

Jimmy grinned and dashed around to the driver's side, leaving Walt shaking his head and still smiling.

The kid couldn't help growing up with a father who was a wizard with numbers, and a mother who could make words sit right up and sing to the point they brought tears to your eyes. Walt knew them both, and respected what they did.

He hadn't spent his whole life with his head buried down inside an engine by any means. He'd spent some of his college years studying on computers, and he was glad of it all the time.

Especially in weather like this, he didn't mind one little bit working inside and getting the town's records updated.

But he was even more glad he'd come up with a whole family full of people who loved to tinker and fix things. He'd learned from both his parents, all four grandparents, aunts and uncles, and more than a few cousins.

The automotive training he had made a huge difference, sure. Walt knew that even at his own tender young age of twenty-six, his habit of paying close attention and figuring things out made him seem like a much older, more experienced man.

Especially to a kid who had the bones of a good mechanic, once he got a good bit more experience and practice.

And built up his confidence most of all.

The choppy rumble of the engine started right up, along with a hit of gas cutting through the clean air. When Jimmy just about bounced back around in front of the truck, Walt's determination to pass along that tinkering habit jumped right back up to full strength.

Then Jimmy got out his smartphone and flipped on the light, and Walt did his best not to wince at the thought of dropping a fancy pocket computer into a running motor. It would take at least a hundred of the little penlights he had in his own pocket to buy a new one of those phones. Walt kept his own older model of the same phone zipped safe and sound in one of his coverall pockets at times like this.

That might be a lesson the kid had to learn for himself.

The light traveled along all the wires and belts and lines, and Walt saw Jimmy's face brighten when he started tracing the smaller, stiff vacuum hoses.

Sure enough, Jimmy darted one hand in and grabbed the tiny loose hose Walt had spotted pretty much from the get go. It was a tricky one for sure, barely as thick as a pencil and sitting snugged up *almost* where it was supposed to be.

Jimmy plucked it up, popped his thumb over it to test the draw, and grinned fit to split. He pushed the hose back down and nodded as the engine smoothed itself out at once.

"There you *go!*" he said, slapping Walt's shoulder with only a little bit too much of a jolt. "Sounds to me like that's got it fixed right up. You're about the best teacher there ever was, Walt. I sure do hope you know that."

Walt blinked and shook his head, then stepped back out of the way so Jimmy could grab his toolbox and slam the hood.

"I reckon you would have worked it out for yourself without me hanging over your shoulder. We all start from somewhere."

Jimmy set the toolbox down on the snowy grass with a thump, then put his hands on his hips.

"See, that there's the trick," he said. "You point

me in the right direction and let me go without making me feel like a damn fool. Starting to think I *might* not have to bug you about something every other day after enough time goes by. Anyway, let me get out of here and you get out of this nasty weather."

Jimmy grabbed his toolbox, dashed back around the front of the truck, and jumped in before Walt could do more than raise his hand. And before he could strongly suggest Jimmy skip his usual gossip-jawing stops on his rounds with a storm coming in. His sociable nature was one reason pretty much everyone in Wolf Branch loved him, after all, and he always got his work done in plenty of time.

This wasn't the night for chit-chat, though.

Still, Walt would have to take Jimmy's compliment as a sign that he was done with teaching for the day, and even more important, that he'd earned the contents of that dinner bucket inside out of the cold.

The deeper truth that he hardly ever admitted to himself was he *knew* way down deep in his bones that Jimmy would come to good, and that Walt was the one to help him get there. Not because he just happened to like the kid, but that didn't hurt.

Walt had strong, deep hunches about people, and sometimes those hunches even came through in his dreams. He'd never known those hunches to be wrong, any more than he'd known the same from his mother and uncles.

So no matter how goofy and downright hopeless Jimmy might seem every once in a while, Walt had *seen* him making a fine mechanic, and a fine father and husband along the way in years to come.

That was more than enough to shore up Walt's patience when it threatened to wear thin.

He ambled toward the glass door of the red brick town hall, stomping and brushing at his shoulders as he climbed the concrete steps to keep from tracking too much melting snow inside. Hopefully he'd have time to feed his grumbling belly before someone else out in the garage—or already out running the roads —showed up needing his help.

A young woman with her long brunette hair piled on top of her head in a messy bun was just putting on her coat to walk out. Linda Burns had been a few years behind Walt in school, but she'd taken to college life natural as you please. He hardly ever saw her much around town except during her holiday breaks, and it seemed like she always wore some variety of jeans and a gray t-shirt.

Today it was from her college over in Hidden Springs instead of the high school in Wolf Branch.

Linda shook her head, but she was smiling as Walt hung his own coat on a row of hooks by the glass front door.

"That boy had you out in the snow listening to

him run his mouth so long I was afraid you'd freeze solid."

Walt laughed and kept going, stepping around behind the cluttered steel desk sitting against one wall. Unlike the desks behind the chest-high counter to the left, it seemed everyone who worked for the town shared this one. The collection of paper, ink pens, keys, and random missing hats and gloves made it just about useless.

The only thing worth getting to was the computer that showed the feed from the town's dispatcher and not much else.

"Jimmy's all right," Walt said, glancing at the monitor. All clear for now. "Just needs a little guidance, that's all. I think he'll turn into a real good mechanic by the time it's all said and done."

"Maybe," Linda said, wrapping a bright blue scarf around her neck and over her static-lively hair. "All I know is you've got the patience for it, more than I ever will."

Walt lowered himself into the rickety old wooden rolling chair, way too short for his lanky frame to begin with, even before it endured years of abuse.

"You say that now, Linda, but I hear you're looking to teach high school when you're finished with your own schooling. I expect a room full of Jimmys will test your patience a lot more than one at a time tests mine."

Linda smiled and held up one hand.

"I hope to teach all right, but not in a big room full of crowded desks and bored kids. I was in back talking to the school superintendent and the mayor about setting up classes at the cannery, for one thing. Teach them some skills they'll be able to use instead of letting all that knowledge die out."

"Now *there's* an idea I can sure get behind, making sure people know how to do pickling and canning right. I hope the town did too." Walt pulled his gunmetal-gray dinner bucket out from under the desk. It was the same kind of big rectangular box his grandfather and father had carried, with the domed lid shaped just right for a thermos full of something hot on a chilly day like this. "You ever taste my Granny Holbrook's dill pickle relish?"

He flipped the top open and pulled out a small plastic container about the size of Linda's fist. As soon as he twisted the light-blue lid off, the sharp aroma of dill and vinegar filled the air.

Linda laughed when Walt's stomach set to growling out loud this time, but she stepped forward and accepted a sample of shining green and red cubes on a green hard plastic travel spoon, the kind with a fork on the other end.

"Don't worry about the spoon," he said, "I keep three or four of them in here all the time."

She breathed in and smiled, then popped the whole thing into her mouth.

"That *is* good, Walt. More spicy than my people make, but just exactly enough to make my taste buds sit up and take notice without lighting me up. Listen, you think your Granny might be willing to do some teaching? I know it's asking an awful lot for her to give up her special recipe, but I'm hoping folks will want to pass their secrets along to the next generations."

"I think you'll find she'd be tickled silly if you asked her. She's been making a point of teaching all us grandkids, so we can make it for her and give her a rest, she says. I can't imagine her ever giving her canning up, to tell you the honest truth."

Linda nodded as she handed the spoon back.

"Okay, now you're giving me some real good ideas about how to get things set up. That's the next step, putting together my presentation for the high school and the cannery. I can just see bringing in more than adults and high school kids for special days with *all* our grandparents. Younger kids can even help with some parts of it. We could put together some of what they all make to share with folks who are down on their luck for whatever reason, get more people and even businesses involved that way."

Walt nodded and popped his thermos loose, hoping the coffee inside was still plenty hot.

"I like that idea, letting kids see how to help. Might be able to get them into gardening some, too."

Linda grinned and stepped back, pulling on a pair of bright pink gloves.

"That's just the kind of thinking we need around here. I'll end up setting you up front and center in one of these committee meetings yet."

She ducked out the door and into the thickening snow before Walt could get out a proper response. He figured something along the lines of "Don't you *dare!*" would be fitting.

"See if I talk to my Granny now," he muttered to himself, trying not to smile, "unless it's to encourage her to keep her secrets to herself."

He pulled out the rest of his lunch and settled in to hush his belly up, wondering how long before he had to start dodging Linda's invitations to speak in front of a great crowd of people.

And wondering even more at how a quiet little part of him thought that kind of speaking would be a grand idea as long as the crowd didn't get *too* big. He didn't have to think too hard on it to know that was his hunches and dreams talking to him.

He'd given up trying to pretend that part of him wasn't the smartest a long, long time ago.

Walt barely finished with the last piece of heavenly fried chicken when a line of bright red text popped up on the dispatcher screen. He leaned forward to read and frowned, reaching for the old-fashioned black desk phone. It rang before he could pick it up.

"Town hall, I'm guessing this is dispatch calling?"

"Yeah, Walt, course it's dispatch," a deep voice with a long, slow drawl said. "Who else expects someone to be sitting there in the town hall this late on a snow night?"

Harry Mullins, putting on his own family's musical mountain accent like he often did when he was home from college. That was another one who had bigger things in mind than riding a small-town dispatch desk on his Christmas vacation, and Walt figured Harry would make it happen here or somewhere else.

He hoped his feeling it would be right there in Wolf Branch turned out to be true.

"I wasn't exactly planning to be here long," Walt said. "I was headed back to the garage to see if anyone needs help getting more snowplows ready. But if someone has managed to skid themselves off the road or something, I'll sure see to that instead."

Harry slipped back into his normal way of talking, somehow sounding much more like a flat-voiced news broadcaster than a boy who grew up running the same backroads and hollers as Walt did.

"Someone running off the road any of us could deal with. Trouble is none of us can raise Jimmy

Adams on the radio or his phone or any other way. He was supposed to check on the road down by the reservoir and the waterworks, make sure no one's parked down there in the way in case someone's water goes out. He never showed up after he left here. Think his truck might have broken down? He's been complaining about it all day."

Walt shook his head, then tucked the phone between his head and shoulder so he could gather up all his lunch things. A shiver had set in all over his body, making his hands shake and jitter something awful.

"He got his truck fixed up before he headed out. I saw him do it. Let me get finished up here, and I'll go out to the reservoir and check. Was he supposed to be heading anywhere else this evening?"

"Just along the usual trouble spots. Bridges and such, and the two big curves heading out of town. Cell reception isn't the greatest in most of those spots, but I figured he would have checked in after he stopped at the water plant."

"Anyone driving a salt truck or plow hear from him?" Walt tucked his dinner bucket back under the desk and stood, wishing his belly wasn't quite so full with the way it was kicking up worried. "Or report seeing anyone off the road? Maybe whoever's on at the water processing plant tonight?"

"Not a word so far, and I haven't been able to get

Sonny Salyers down at the water plant. That's nothing new, though. He's pretty good at getting caught up in whatever book he takes down there with him and missing everything but a knock on the door as long as none of the machines seize up. That or running his mouth. But it all runs without a hitch when he's there, and he can fix things no one else can figure out."

Harry breathed in deep, then blew out loud enough that Walt held the phone away from his ear.

"Anyway, I'll ping all of them on the radio again soon as we hang up," Harry said. "I'll send out anyone who has a safe vehicle to drive in this mess too. You be careful out there, Walt. This snow might not be as bad as they predicted just yet, but with all the rain lately there's likely to be black ice. We don't want two of you skidding out."

"I got my own four-wheel drive, and chains if I need 'em. Do me a favor and hold off on sending any more plows out for a bit if you can. I'd hate for them to cover over the very tracks we might need if he did go off the road. I'm heading out right now."

Walt shook his head as he shrugged back into his coat, adding a thick red scarf around his head and neck, and matching gloves. All a gift from his parents when he started work for the town, along with the heavy work boots.

Silly as Jimmy could be, Walt had never known

him to be a careless driver in any kind of weather. But like anyone just barely nineteen, he didn't hardly have enough behind-the-wheel experience to tell for sure.

When Walt stepped outside, he let out a low whistle. The temperature had to have dropped a good ten degrees, maybe fifteen since the sun disappeared behind the ridge, and the snow was gathering itself to fall with a purpose now. Big, heavy flakes falling straight down to join up with a couple of inches already on the ground. Linda's footprints on the sidewalk were already gone, along with her tire tracks.

All he could see of Wolf Branch was the white halos of the street lights, and only the closest ones of those.

Bad news for anyone to be caught out on a night like this. And Walt couldn't pretend he didn't feel at least a little bit responsible for sending Jimmy out.

The kid hadn't asked, and Walt wasn't his supervisor at any rate.

But still, Walt had helped him get his truck fixed up, and this storm had all the makings of a bad one.

Walt started up his trusty old Jeep instead of one of the town's vehicles, then stepped back out to knock the worst of the snow off the windshield. Better in a case like this to get behind the wheel of something he knew inside and out.

His mind worked a mile a minute, thinking through all the places Jimmy might have gone and gotten himself into trouble.

Nothing for it except to get out there and see.

But Walt would have to find his way along the roads himself before he could help anyone else. Even on roads he'd traveled his whole life long, that was going to be a challenge tonight.

He'd barely gotten himself out of town and across the highway toward the reservoir, and already his eyes were feeling the strain of trying to look through a million huge snowflakes swirling in all directions.

Slowing down to barely a crawl didn't help much, but he was afraid to go much faster. Thank the good sense of most folks in Wolf Branch he didn't see anyone else out and about. But that didn't mean he wouldn't come up on a vehicle skidded off to the side that he *didn't* expect, no matter how hard he was hoping to see some trace of Jimmy's green truck

And even though he knew most animals were smarter than people on a night like this, the thought of running some critter down kept him backing off on the gas pedal.

He finally bumped onto the rough-graveled reservoir road, feeling and hearing the change as the tires crunched into snow with no pavement underneath it.

Feeling the *other* change too, the one that was a

hell of a lot harder to explain to anyone outside of his own family. Even under his t-shirt, flannel shirt, coveralls, and jacket, Walt's hair tried to stand on end all over his arms.

One of his hunches getting strong enough to break through into the real world and his own flesh and blood.

Even if Jimmy wasn't out here somewhere, Walt needed to be paying real close attention to something.

Without street lights to navigate by and the road ahead a uniform white blanket, he slowed even more, eyes darting from side to side trying to see everything at once. He didn't need any kind of fancy GPS or phone to remember the gradual curve ahead as it wrapped around toward the town's water processing plant.

Wolf Branch was small enough that a couple of low brick buildings with most of the workings hidden away down below was all it took, perched beside a treatment area that wasn't much more than a glorified pond. The problem from his perspective right that second was the way both sides of the road held a steep drop-off that would be way too easy to miss with rotten visibility.

A drop that went straight into the reservoir and the assembly of pipes and pumps laid out across it on one side.

Down the rocky slope built up years ago for the road itself on the other, ending in the boulder-filled waterfalls of the Grasppe River itself about twenty feet down. A river running high and fast—and icy cold—after all the rain over the past couple of weeks.

Neither one a good place to end up if you didn't mean to on a sunny summer day, much less on a winter night with snow piling up.

None of that stopped kids with cars and people they wanted to spend *private* time with from gathering all along the long arc of the road, and Walt couldn't hardly blame them for that. When the trees and brush had their spectacular leaves on in spring, summer, and autumn, and even in winter when the branches were bare, this was a right pretty part of town. The falls themselves were reason enough, though folks could get a better view from considerably less-secluded hiking trails.

Add that to hardly anyone besides the water plant's caretaker coming out here once they grew up and had better arrangements for privacy, and he understood the draw. After all, he'd kept time on this very road with a partner or two during his own high school days.

He'd never known the prickly warning now working its way over his legs and back as well as his arms to be wrong before. But no one was out here tonight, and he didn't see any signs that Jimmy or anyone else had slipped over the sides of the road, either.

Walt paused at the broad circular cleared area at the end of the road, where he could swing around (carefully) and drive back out toward the highway. Then head toward the bridges Jimmy might have been on his way to check out. The only other option was a road that cut down at a sharp angle to his right and ended at the water plant's tiny square of a parking lot. Too steep an angle to risk tonight unless he had a good reason to.

He stared, eyes pointed toward the windshield. But he didn't really see the snow building up, getting swept aside by his wipers, then building up again. Or hear the soft *scree* that meant those wiper blades had seen better days.

He was paying more attention to what was going on inside than out.

And still getting that tingling sense that something was wrong right where he was.

He pulled off one glove so he could get out his cell phone with fingers not quite numb, but close. The only problem with the Jeep on a night like this was it took about half-past forever for the inside to warm up. Most of the time, Walt got where he was going before he got anywhere near good and toasty.

A couple of quick taps, and he held the warm

phone to his cold face and ear. Harry Mullins answered right away.

"You got him, Walt?"

"No, sorry to say I haven't seen a trace of Jimmy or anyone else out here. You able to raise anyone yet? Sonny out here at the water plant, maybe?"

"No one who could tell me anything new. And nothing from Sonny. Think it's safe to go down there? That road's a slippery mess when it rains."

Walt nodded to himself, and his eyes drifted to the right. Where the road seemed to drop off into nothing.

"Don't think it's safe at all, no. But I got a real strong feeling I need to get myself down there and check it out."

Harry was quiet for a minute, no doubt thinking about the fact that he wasn't Walt's supervisor any more than Walt was Jimmy's. And probably wishing he could think of a good reason to say no.

"I know you got your Jeep and all," Harry said, slipping back into the local accent more than he usually did. "And I know you grew up driving in winter weather just like all the rest of us did. Still, gravels can get slippery as glass with snow packed down on them. Can you at least give me a call when you get down there, Walt? And take a minute to put your chains on if it's the least little bit slick getting back out?"

Decision made—partly because Harry's words really did sound like permission—Walt slipped the Jeep into four-wheel drive low gear with his free hand.

"Will do, Harry, I promise. What I'll probably find is Sonny bundled up snug as a cat, everything running fine, and him wondering why on earth I'm bothering him when he thought he'd got a quiet night all to himself for reading."

"Probably so. Let me know either way."

Walt put his glove back on and stretched his fingers out, trying to loosen up the bad-weather-driving tension. Then he slowly turned the steering wheel toward the little spur road going down to the water plant.

In that moment, it didn't matter one bit that he knew exactly where he should aim. Or that he could see the slight dip in the snow where the road was.

His heart sped up and he breathed a mite faster when it looked like the front end of his Jeep was pointed toward a fast trip to nowhere fun.

When his headlights finally swept down instead of pointing up into almost solid white, Walt's relief didn't last long. Instead of seeing the green bulk of Jimmy's truck tucked in beside Sonny's little burgundy Subaru, he only saw the Subaru.

"Where in the hell did you get to, Jimmy?" he muttered under his breath.

He stopped with his headlights now shining strong against the water plant's brick wall and a solid blue metal door, thinking he should just back right up out of there and keep on looking. Odds were high Sonny would never know Walt had been there with no windows on this side, and the snow would cover up the tire tracks soon enough.

On the chance Jimmy had already been here and Sonny might know where he was headed next, Walt turned off the engine and climbed out.

Right back into heavier snow and a good, stiff wind to drive the cold even deeper into his bones.

Several thumps of his gloved hand on the door didn't rouse Sonny, which put a little bit more of an edge on Walt's case of the jitters. Much as he hated to go charging in and startle someone, he pulled his glove off again, grimacing when the wind took a nasty bite.

Thank goodness the key he needed was the biggest one on the ring, and the light over the doorway was close enough to see by even in the heavy snow.

He shoved the door open and stepped into a short, dim hallway.

"Sonny? Walt Colley here, nothing to worry about. Sonny?"

Nothing but the faint hum of pumps and

machinery, and the chlorine smell that never quite went away.

That and an odor of...exhaust, maybe?

Not the usual thing in here, but maybe Sonny was working on one of the older, ornery units.

The floor, walls, and ceiling of the small room were dark gray concrete, and the overhead banks of glaring fluorescent light were switched off. Like they generally were when nothing was going wrong, but the deep shadows didn't relax Walt's neck and shoulders one little bit.

That hunch had worked itself up into more of a knot now, one that took hold of his belly to go along with his muscles and chest.

"Sonny? Call out if you can hear me."

The monitoring station with its desk and computer displays to the right was empty, same as Sonny's usual perch in a battered old easy chair with a table and a reading light to the left. A series of pipes and tubes and gauges spread out from the monitoring station along the wall in front of Walt, all of them leading to the stairs that went down to the equipment room below.

Through a door Sonny almost always kept closed unless something was going wrong.

Tonight the black metal door stood open, and the bright lights in the stairwell were on.

Walt headed that way, his nose wrinkling at the stronger exhaust stink.

Strong enough to make the air feel oily and thick.

He was still a few feet away from the door when he spotted an outstretched arm wearing a red and blue flannel shirt.

"Sonny!"

Walt dashed forward, kneeling and touching Sonny's winter-pale neck where his shoulder-length gray hair had fallen aside.

When Sonny drew back from the cold touch, Walt let out a gusty breath so hard he almost fell down the metal steps himself.

"The hell you been eating, Walt?" Sonny said in a weak voice, eyes still closed. "Smell like a pickle barrel."

"Since you don't reek like you've been hitting the holiday cheer early," Walt said with a laugh, "want to tell me why you're laid out on the steps like that?"

Sonny rolled one red-rimmed eye open.

"*Hell* no I ain't been drinking. Quit all that nonsense near twenty years ago. Help me sit up, 'bout to freeze solid here."

Walt took a few steps down, taking care to avoid the sprawl of arms and legs. The hum of machinery below sounded about right, but the exhaust stink was stronger. He lifted the much smaller man and helped him get to his reading chair

"What happened, Sonny? Got a motor having trouble down there?"

Sonny lifted a shaking hand and rubbed at his forehead. Walt opened the warm, half-full bottle of Coca-Cola on the table beside a stack of books and held it so Sonny could take a few swallows. Even flat, that much sugar and caffeine might help clear his head a little.

"Probably turn out it was worse trouble than I realized," Sonny said, shaking his head. "Had a pump act like it was taking a clog, so I went down to clear it out. Took me longer than I thought. Started to come over all dizzy and kinda puny, head aching like back in my bad drinking days. Made it to where you found me before I had to take a little rest."

"Sounds to me like the ventilation is what took a clog." Walt walked over and closed the door before he picked up the old-fashioned black desk phone's handset at the monitoring station. "I'm no doctor, but I think you got a lungful of carbon monoxide going there."

Sonny tried to laugh and ended up hacking out a bunch of coughs at the same time as Harry Mullins answered back at the town hall.

"Sonny? 'Bout damn time you called in. You got Jimmy Adams or Walt Colley out there with you?"

"This here's Walt, Harry. I suspect what Sonny's got is a good dose of carbon monoxide poisoning, but he's awake and all now. I'm going to get him out to the hospital before the roads get any worse. Hang on."

Walt held the phone against his chest.

"You seen Jimmy down here tonight, Sonny, or heard from him?"

Sonny shook his head and reached for his Coke, this time without nearly the shakes he had before.

"Not a whisper from him. What's that goofy kid gone and gotten himself into now?"

Before Walt could answer, the entry door swung open with a blast of frigid air and snow, and Jimmy Adams himself swept into the little room.

"Y'all having a party and forget to invite... *Sonny?* You all right?"

Walt lowered his chin to his chest and blew with his cheeks puffed out. He held the phone to his ear.

"That's Jimmy just walked in, looking nothing but a bit chilly around the edges. Listen, Harry, there's a problem down here with one of the motors, but it just might have to wait until this storm blows itself out. I'm gonna help Sonny and send Jimmy back to you."

Walt watched Jimmy crouch beside Sonny, patting Sonny's arm while pointing the bright light from his smartphone into one eye, then the other.

"Don't be too hard on him, Harry," Walt said in a quiet voice. "He looks a good ways past scared half to death, but he's checking on Sonny first thing. We'll get it all figured out."

"I guess so, now that we know where he is," Harry said. "You take care getting out of there. And thank you. I'm awful glad you went by the water plant when you did. I'll get the word out to everyone to stay away until we can get someone in there and figure out what went wrong."

Walt turned to hear Sonny fussing at Jimmy, but he sounded more pleased than annoyed.

"I guess I just *told* you I'm okay. Might not be if I'd laid there much longer, but I'll do for now."

Jimmy turned to Walt, his eyes wide and upset.

"I should have stopped by here first thing, Walt, I can't *believe* I did that."

"Hang on now, everything's going to be just fine. I do have to ask where you went that took you so long."

Hands on his hips and staring at the concrete floor, Jimmy shook his head.

"I got it into my damn fool head that I'd be better off checking the bridges and such first. You know, before the snow got too bad. I heard my phone light up when I got back in range of a cell tower, but I figured I'd deal with that once I got inside here." He looked up, and now his eyes were edged with red, too.

"I'm real sorry to upset everyone."

Sonny snorted. "You won't find me complaining about that, Jimmy. I guess I'm just about the worst one in town for not paying attention to my phone, anyone will tell you. Don't you beat yourself up over something that all came out right in the end. Or it will soon as the doctors pump me full of oxygen or something like that."

Jimmy looked up, but his lips were pressed tight together. He opened his mouth but Walt jumped in instead.

"Sonny's right about that. I need to get him out to the hospital to get seen to, and you need to get back to the town hall. We're going to lock up here for the night and worry about it when the roads are clear, right Sonny?"

"Why sure," Sonny said, waving one hand toward the closed door to the stairs. "I got that clog sorted out, and someone needs to bring a respirator in here to check on the rest. Everything ought to run fine for now."

Walt patted Jimmy's shoulder and smiled.

"Why don't you help me load him in the Jeep? Might need to put the chains on if the road's too much of a mess. And don't let Harry give you too much of a hard way to go. I'll tell you some tales on him sometime, from back in high school before he got all official."

Jimmy stared at Walt for a few seconds, then he finally laughed.

"Sounds good to me. Come on, Sonny, let's get you out of here and I'll get back to the town hall for whatever I got coming. If it's an ass-chewing after all, I'll want to hear those stories about Harry for sure."

Walt gathered up Sonny's books and let Jimmy take care of Sonny's jacket, gloves, scarf, and Sonny himself.

As he locked the water plant door tight behind him, he barely felt the shock of the cold.

The snow had turned more gentle and slow for now, and just as beautiful as anything he could imagine floating down past the light above the doorway.

And Walt's hunch had shifted itself from worried and scared into calm and happy.

Which was just exactly where he liked to be.

KARI KILGORE

AUTHOR OF THE SOUND OF MURDER AND TERMINALIA

Andre's Extra-Sensational Adventure

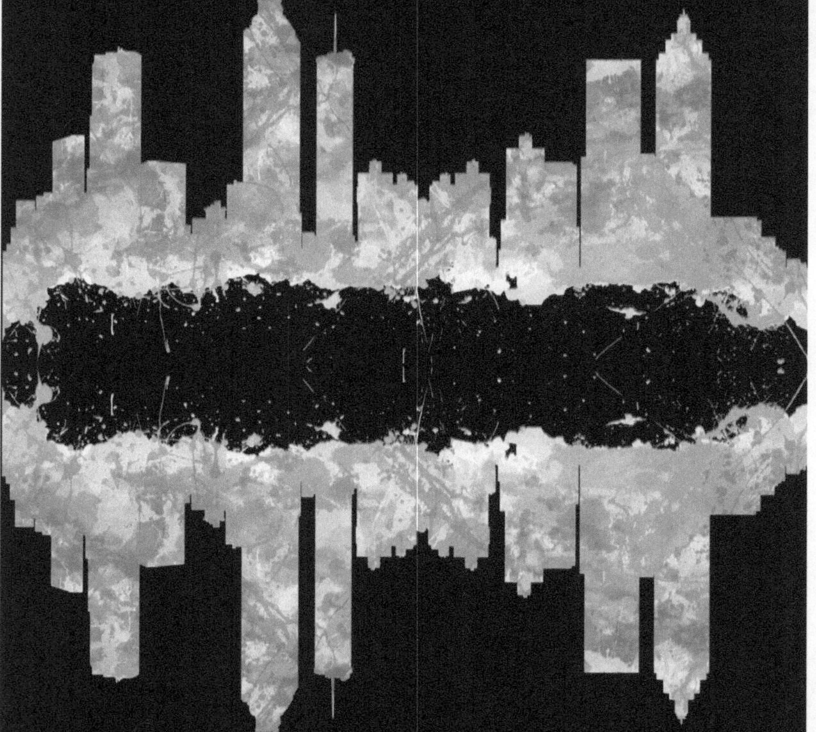

*For anyone who's ever had an adventure
while pet sitting*

CHAPTER 1

Andre Telkin adored the groovy old neighborhoods on the east side of Atlanta, any time of day or night, and pretty much every day of the year.

Wide graceful streets, with huge oak and pine and maple trees everywhere. Even after dark and early in Georgia's blink-and-you-miss-it springtime, the massive tree trunks in yards and along sidewalks added a solid sense of an established home. All that green kept the air smelling fresh and clean rather than choked up with the stink of too many people, not to mention the few gas-burners still roaming the highways.

Some of the streets were even divided by a strip of grass, flowers, and trees down the middle. All those miniature gardens were tastefully decorated and maintained, of course, with the whole community pitching in. Most of them featured a few patches of early vegetables and herbs for everyone to share.

Something no one would ever see in the cookie-cutter, soulless hell of subdivisions north of the city.

The other thing that couldn't be more different from the distant suburbs was the houses themselves. Nothing modern or predictable here, and certainly not identical to the point of requiring a trail of bread-crumbs to find your way around.

These houses were well over a hundred years old, built long before the days of swarms of cute little e-cars and the growing CommuShare system that linked more and more of the sprawling city together. Mostly adorable Craftsman bungalows, made of wood or brick, and just bursting with style and character that certain areas of *newer* Atlanta were in desperate need of.

Original wavy glass windows, and broad porches out front for sitting pretty or keeping an eye out for good neighborhood gossip. Classic lap-board siding on the wood ones that looked fabulous in about every paint shade under the sun.

Andre stepped out of his own fierce little e-car, brilliant purple with flawless copper upholstery. When he needed a can't-miss mood boost, he dressed himself to match, right down to the swoops and whorls he kept trimmed into his close-cut, tightly curled black hair.

Those copper highlights worked beautifully with his dark skin, which he was never afraid to play up to its fullest.

One thing he *had* been afraid to play up not all that long ago rested right behind his left ear, and tonight it gave him yet another reason to love this old neighborhood. His cochlear implant was only about the size of a pea, and it had been simple for him to grow his hair long enough to keep it covered for years.

But now he trimmed his hair up above it on purpose, and he'd even built up quite a collection of sparkly covers to work with his every outfit, whim, and mood.

A change he credited his best friend Dana for, no matter how hard she fussed and tried to deflect when he brought it up.

He'd helped Dana solve a tricky fraud case a while back, mainly through the bionic-level hearing his implant provided. That and the protection it provided from a nasty subliminal message that convinced a bunch of people to off themselves.

He'd never been a huge fan of typical self-improvement guru stuff, but he'd never expected it could turn deadly.

In any case, once Andre gave Dana that assist, the

hair shield slipped into the past. And he took to playing up his implant as the spectacular asset it truly was.

An asset that enjoyed the deep peace and quiet of Dana's neighborhood immensely after the hustle and traffic and noise of a typical Atlanta day.

He headed up the rising driveway toward one of those gorgeous old houses—this one still painted a sadly ordinary reddish brown that stood out in the soft light from the streetlamps. He expected that tragic color to change before too much more time passed. After all, Dana never even tried to dispute how much she needed Andre's input when it came to fashion and style, not to mention general good taste.

He'd get her to liven up this place with an updated color palette for sure.

She just needed to remember that when it came to such things, Andre always knew best.

He stopped on the short walkway going toward the front porch, right before he put one foot on the concrete steps.

Sure enough, he heard the wailing song of the feline people.

Horribly neglected, they cried. Left alone forever and ever in the big, empty house.

Cruelly confined, with no means of gathering up the massive amounts of attention they routinely demanded, and deserved.

And most importantly, and implausibly, the wailers claimed they were surely on the edge of starvation, since they hadn't been fed for years.

Years!

Andre snorted and shook his head as he walked up the stairs. He didn't need his electronically enhanced hearing to pick up all that noise and foolishness.

And he knew before he ever opened the door that Dana's spoiled-pitifully-rotten cats likely had enough food and water to last them for at least three more days.

The cats had hurtled themselves into their dirge-singing ways a mere seven hours after she headed out of town.

He opened the screen door and stepped onto the porch, laughing out loud at the way the caterwauling stopped in an instant.

"Oh *yes*, babies," he said. "Your grand rescuer has arrived. Just give Uncle Andre a second to bust down this door and deliver you from your eternal confinement."

He couldn't see the porch in the dim light from the street, and Dana had stubbornly refused any kind of motion light for out here. She hated the thought of her own house blinding her before she even got inside.

But the porch was one way Andre knew his

exceedingly patient and terribly generous influence was getting through to his stylistically challenged friend. The wood slats of the swing were freshly painted a sparkling midnight blue, with cushions covered in all the constellations. He'd even gotten her to let him paint the swing's chains in glittering silver.

Once he conquered the porch, the rest of the house would fall under his obviously superior influence in no time.

Andre held his hand in front of the invisible sensor built into the doorknob, waiting for its beyond-typical-human-hearing hum to shift from a rough and high-pitched "Excuse me, do I know you?" to a lower, smooth "Welcome friend, come on inside!"

After the switch, he hesitated, hand on the cool metal doorknob with its welcoming faint green glow.

Between the still-silent cats and the lowered noise from the sensor, he heard something else. Something new that hadn't been here any of the many other times he'd graced Dana's house with his presence.

An unsettling, modulating noise, one that almost...*churned*, like a huge, obnoxious fan that was out of balance, lurking somewhere outside the house and cutting through the quiet. Andre had never heard anything quite like it, but he had no reason to believe it was sinister.

Just strange.

But he couldn't quite shake the feeling that it didn't belong.

An especially plaintive yowl from right on the other side of the door broke his contemplation, and he was amazed it didn't shatter the windows all along the front of the house, too.

"Lord have *mercy*, you fussy little beasts. I'm right here."

He stepped inside, into a circulating frenzy of feline misery and hopeful excitement. One short-haired black cat, leggy and slender with an altogether too-long tail, and one compact, long-haired black cat, who made up for her smaller size with a much louder mouth.

The two sweet, gorgeous creatures who'd waited lonely and unwanted for ages because of an absurd superstition about their glossy black fur had caught Dana's eye the second she walked through the shelter door a few months back. Andre had been by her side, silently rooting for the outcasts who deserved love and attention every bit as much as the more showy purebred types.

A dynamic he and Dana both understood in their bones, and a huge reason they'd been best friends pretty much since the day they met.

"Okay, beauties, tell Uncle Andre all about the horrors you've endured in this perfectly fine little house just crammed full of your toys and beds and about a thousand pounds of crazy expensive cat food and kitty nibbles. And I'll pass along every single one of your tales of woe to Uncle Henry, don't you worry."

He knelt on the hardwood floor of Dana's living room, wishing his new boyfriend wasn't out of town on a photography assignment, *and* the same week as Dana. That was certainly unfair, and it really should be illegal by someone's measure besides his own.

To make things even more intolerable, after tonight Henry's Savannah gig would be entirely from dusk to dawn. And Andre worked his unbelievably cool (and geeky) lab job through all the daylight hours, when Henry would be snoozing.

They'd barely have time for more than a tuck-you-in-to-sleep text message, or maybe a sweet and sexy video or several.

He consoled himself by busily reassuring long-legged Jimi and short-legged Fizgig, regaling them with his own tale of woe while keeping his opinions about how the rainbow of cat accessories and necessities provided most of the kick and flair in the otherwise bland room. Tan walls, brown sofa and chairs, and not a flashy rug or piece of art or even a glamorous light fixture to be seen.

"Don't you worry, babies. We'll get this place fixed up to your standards, and mine, before much longer. Maybe when Mama Dana gets back from her latest hot-shot investigator trip, we can convince her to spend her appropriately huge bonus on this place. Then Uncle Henry can take care of the photo shoot, and we'll sell it as decorating advice for the hopelessly bland everywhere."

He stood, hands on his hips, giggling as the cats wrapped themselves into contortions, swirling around his legs.

"Now show me how much you've been starved, and I'll hold my nose and clean up all the evidence that you've been eating like sweet little silky pigs so no one will *dare* call you liars."

An hour of tidying and feeding and lavishing mutual adoration all around later, Andre stepped back onto the porch. He'd been tempted to snuggle down for the night with the kitties, and Dana had made it clear the offer was open.

On the other hand, Henry's incredibly sweet and appreciative pit bull Daisy Girl waited for her own dose of snuggling and attention, even though Andre had already stopped by Henry's place a few hours before.

Yes, of course dogs needed to go out more often, and Daisy was an absolute sweetheart. Combine that with Henry's a-*ma*-zing loft apartment/photography studio, and yeah, the fact that his relationship with Henry was far more intimate than his with Dana.

Or at least differently intimate, since Andre honestly couldn't remember the last time he hadn't told Dana about anything. Including Henry.

Either way, with profuse apologies to his feline devotees, he closed the door and re-armed the security system. Thankfully the cats showed their appreciation by letting him go with only a couple of sweet chirps rather than more banshee howls.

Andre pretended they were sitting by the door, pining for his return, when he knew they were probably already on their way to one of a dozen fancy cat beds with their bellies stuffed full.

When he closed the screen door behind him and stepped out into the night, that bizarre churning noise caught his attention once again.

It wasn't louder, exactly, and it didn't sound any closer. Partly because he was having trouble pinning down what direction it came from.

But it did sound more discordant somehow to his highly sensitive and well-trained bionic ear. Like the noise had turned up the volume, or the speed, only emphasizing whatever was unnatural and out of balance in the first place.

Andre walked down the steps and back to his e-car, turning his head from side to side, probably looking almost as adorable as Daisy Girl tilting her beautiful blocky head to the left or right.

A tiny bit—not exactly stronger, but more clearly resolved—to the east, maybe? Facing the same direction as his car did, parallel to Dana's house. But he couldn't see a thing moving down that way. Only more of the same fantastic bungalows, with their owners either settled in or still out for the night.

He took a few steps forward before his phone buzzed in his pocket and his watch buzzed on his wrist, and the alert piped directly into his implant started up. Henry's pre-recorded voice whispering "Hey there handsome. Want to hear a secret?"

Andre grinned as he raised his watch to see Henry's own handsome face winking at him.

He glanced down the street toward the weird noise, then tapped the watch to answer Henry's call. If the noise was still there in the morning or tomorrow night, he'd check it out then.

For now, far more important—and pleasant— duties called.

"Hello there, you gorgeous man," he said. "Tell me how wonderful it is down there in Savannah, then tell me how much you miss me. Because I miss *you* to an embarrassing degree and I'm not ready to fess up just yet."

CHAPTER 2

ANDRE COULDN'T CATCH a trace of the strange sound the next morning on his fabulous feline visit, not that he'd really expected to. Even Dana's sleepy neighborhood perked up quite a bit when the sun was up on a weekday.

The elementary school on the next block alone contributed an unbelievable amount of noise and energy to the atmosphere, along with a welcome splash of color and style as far as Andre was concerned.

Neither Jimi nor Fizgig were any help at all, possibly because they were too busy bemoaning their night of eternal neglect while he topped up their nearly full food bowls and dispensed treats. Andre returned the favor by explaining how much

Dana missed them (and him), and especially how much she missed spring in Atlanta compared to St. Louis.

He couldn't tell for sure, but he suspected the cats were as horrified by the idea of Dana's adventures in freezing rain as he was.

The second he stepped out of his car that night—when the temperature in Atlanta had dropped to a balmy 68 degrees rather than the heart-chilling below freezing Dana told him about—the maddening sound was louder than the night before. Tonight it reminded him of a gigantic stand mixer with a bearing about to splinter into tiny metal shards.

And that intense feeling of something unnatural, or at least not *usual*, had grown stronger.

He pulled out his phone, then tapped the controls for his implant, switching it from his normal superpower hearing down to a typical person's. Dana's, for example, and Henry's, and most other folks he came across. Andre felt like he'd wrapped a scarf around his head, or maybe pulled down the thick knitted cap he'd surely need to survive even a few hours in the frozen Midwest.

Nope, not a trace of the bizarre churning.

He flipped the levels back to normal, hesitated for a second, then thumbed over and tapped Dana's number. She was hardly a social butterfly under any circumstances, but Andre had mild hopes she at least had a passing knowledge of her neighborhood. He certainly found it at least a thousand times more intriguing and entertaining than her former digs in an apartment complex so vast he was surprised it didn't have its own zip code, post office, and liquor store.

After a couple of rings, leaving Andre full of irrational hope that she'd gone out to explore St. Louis with an exciting companion he'd get to hear all about, Dana answered.

"I'm sure you're calling to tell me more about my drama-queen cats, which I always want to hear more of. As long as you finally admit you encourage their performances with extra treats."

Andre blew her a good raspberry across the miles and electrons. And he didn't fail to notice there was some kind of noise in the background there, too. A general roar of what might actually be conversation, *after* work hours.

Unheard of in Dana-world, at least not without Andre to relentlessly encourage her to get her introverted backside out the door.

"Those rotten thespian children of yours don't need encouragement from me or anyone else to act out the tragic horror of the last forty-eight hours.

And you're the ultimate stage mother accusing me like that. Are you actually out *socializing*? Because I'll need to get somewhere so I can sit down and deal with my case of the vapors if you are."

"Hardly. Or I wouldn't call it socializing, at least, not until you called and I could take the excuse to step outside. I got dragged out to dinner, very much against my will. Great Italian place, but I didn't start working from home the first chance I got because I wanted to hang out with a bunch of insurance types."

Andre shivered. "If you're outside in the depths of Midwestern winter, you *are* desperate."

"You wouldn't *believe* how desperate if I told you. I'm in the lobby, but I'm considering ducking out and walking back to the hotel. Or skating back on what has to be sheets of solid ice by now. They're a brand-new field office, so they don't even have a grumpy database admin or a dorky network admin for me to huddle in the corner with. How are the glamor twins tonight?"

"I haven't gone inside yet, but I can't imagine the ugly hand of fate has turned on them in less than twelve hours. Although that dreary mess you call a décor might be slowly driving them insane. I'm calling because of something going on outside this time. Getting a very strange noise to the east of your place, like the world's biggest bargain store window fan with a truly impressive layer of dust, pollen, and shredded bug bits."

"Nice imagery, Andre. I can just about feel the humidity even though it's dry as a bone up here with all the furnaces going full blast. I haven't heard anything, but I'm guessing you're on bionic mode when you catch it?"

"Sure thing," Andre said, taking a few steps toward the suspicious disturbance. "When I dropped back to Dana levels, the whole thing disappeared. Any intriguing new neighbors that you know of? Or maybe an armada of rhinestone-encrusted drones rehearsing for a drag-themed field show?"

Dana choked back a laugh that he suspected was threatening to get too loud and disorderly in the fancy restaurant that the insurance crew she was training preferred.

"I don't know of anything like that going on, but now I'm not going to rest until I see that field show in person. What are you thinking? Some kind of, I don't know, trouble with utilities or something like that?"

Andre shook his head and kept walking.

"I don't know what I'm thinking, but whatever it is seems to be getting worse. Like it's more and more out of balance, or about to break down. Or tear itself open. This neighborhood is supposed to be all residential, right?"

"Yeah, except for people like me. I'm sure I'm not the only—"

Silence...

"Dana? I think the hazards of all the beautiful but signal-killing trees around here have struck again. You there?"

Andre stopped walking, then froze with his hand halfway into his pocket to grab the phone and check the signal.

It wasn't only the cell phone's sound that had cut out. The silence was far more profound than that.

All the sound in the world around him had gone dead at the same time.

Even the air itself seemed to have stilled.

He looked around, getting his visual bearings like he always did, by falling back on the sense he'd been born with when the sense he'd acquired as a kid slipped for some reason.

Still nothing unusual as far as he could tell. The street was still dim except for the lights overhead and the occasional porch or window light, and nothing moved around him that couldn't be explained by the evening breeze he only barely felt against his skin.

Andre took a few steps backward, raising his phone to eye level. The signal still showed at full strength, with a call connected.

A call that burst back into his awareness when he passed some kind of invisible boundary, along with all the other unremarkable noises and sensations of moving air that only drew attention to themselves when they stopped.

"...catch what you said. Might have hit a rotten spot for signal there."

"I hit a rotten spot all right," he said. "Walked right into a cone of silence about fifty feet away from your house. *Literally* silent for me, I'm more than a little bit freaked out to admit. The call never dropped, but it knocked out my whole processor until I backed myself up and out of it."

He turned to the left and right, marking exactly where he stood. One foot was even with the door handle of a cute little e-car, with the faint light glittering off of thick stands of beads draped around the driver's side headrest for some strange and festive reason. The other foot sat across from a cheery spray of daffodils that had already closed up shop for the evening.

"Your *implant* cut out?" Dana said, surprise clear in her voice now that he could hear her again. "They're hardened against interference, aren't they?"

"For anything that should show up in a residential neighborhood they are. Unless you think someone's running a backyard MRI with the power jacked up to eleven, maybe? Or using the mother of all illegal mobile phone jammers?"

"You see anything that looks like that kind of

operation? As far as I know, everyone who lives there is as boring as me. Where are you, exactly?"

"About three houses down from yours," Andre said, "by your neighbors with the strange but intriguing bead habit going on in their car. Listen, I'm going to tiptoe over the line again and see what happens. I'll keep talking and you do the same."

"Wait, don't you think we should—"

And one half-step plunged him into silence, and that strange numbness.

The phone still showed as connected, and Andre spoke, doing his best not to get too loud without any input from his processor. Only the impression of his own throat and chest vibrating, another of those odd details people never paid attention to.

"Cut out again, just like before."

The same half-step backward.

"...get too close to whatever it is, would you? I heard you the whole time, even though you apparently couldn't hear me telling you to *stop*. But everything is working now?"

"Working like a charm." Andre turned in a slow circle. "Nothing but more of these fantastic bungalows far as the eye can see. Just not as far as the bionic ear can hear. Once I take care of your four-legged divas, I might walk around the block and see how far this goes. You get any new neighbors lately?"

A rustle and mutter came from Dana's end of the

conversation, and Andre wasn't the least bit surprised to hear an aggravated sigh when she spoke again.

"They're wondering where I've run off to, so I guess I should get back in there. No new neighbors that I know of, but you know I'm hardly the keeping-track-of-the-neighbors kind. Hey, don't get too close to whatever it is, okay? Or maybe you should just report it to someone instead."

Andre slowly walked back toward Dana's house and his querulous godkitties, paying close attention to how the weird churning sound rose and fell around him.

"I can't very well get too close to something I can't find, now can I? And as soon as you figure out exactly who I should report it to, I'll get right on that. No one out in the ordinary world, anyway. You need to get back to your fascinating dinner companions, Miss Thing, before they make you get up and do karaoke."

"At least I wouldn't have to listen to the talking if I was singing. If you're thinking about getting in touch with Kelly and Marlene, I say that's a great idea. They've been to my place before, so if you all want to go inside and get comfortable, do whatever makes sense. You *call me* if anything happens, hear? Or if the kitties are terribly in need of me."

"Will do, but I think Fizgig and Jimi will manage

for another day or two with my tender mercies. Now get back in there and chitchat."

He stopped beside his own car, wishing he had a way to record a sound that most people wouldn't be able to hear. Everything still seemed calm around him.

Except even more than the night before, something didn't *feel* right.

A call to Kelly and Marlene might indeed be in order. He and Dana had met them right before New Year's Eve, on one of the rare occasions he'd managed to get Dana out into the world to enjoy an unforgettable party.

Meeting two other people their age who were also in the habit of investigating...unusual occurrences was only the beginning. Kelly and Marlene were in the *business* of the unusual, almost to the point of the unbelievable.

Kelly himself, and herself, turned the highly unlikely into the mind-blowing truth.

And Marlene and Andre shared a knack for hearing things no one else could, even though hers was totally organic.

With the way this bizarre noise got all of Andre's own sense of the strange turned up, getting in touch with Kelly and Marlene might be the only thing that made sense.

Andre walked slowly up the driveway, trying

without any kind of success to push the distracting noise into the background. It broke through even when he concentrated on listening for Fizgig and Jimi's siren song of abandonment and certain starvation.

He hated to admit it all the way down to the soles of his sparkling blue shoes that caught every tiny bit of light, but he wasn't quite comfortable initiating this kind of investigation on his own. Or any other kind of investigation, really.

As a proudly gay hearing-impaired African-American man, Andre hadn't shied away from many challenges in his life. And he'd been fearless and bold in working with Dana on many occasions, including the night the two of them dug into Kelly's background (with permission) and uncovered the carefully constructed dual identities.

But part of that had been following Dana's lead. Responding to her courage in charging forward into an unknown crime.

Doing everything he could to help his best friend.

This would be stepping into his own space, taking the action to figure this crazy thing out. Maybe not a crime, and he truly hoped it wasn't.

Still, making the call on his own felt scarier than he wanted to admit.

Which of course transformed an intimidating

new step into something he was bound and *damned* determined to do.

And the first step was calling on friends who had the best chance to help him do just that.

Decision made and his natural stubborn courage engaged to the fullest, Andre headed up to Dana's house to face his fussy but appreciative feline audience.

CHAPTER 3

Andre wasn't the least bit surprised when Kelly and Marlene agreed to join him that evening. He would have been shocked if they'd turned down the chance to investigate such an odd phenomenon.

After all, they both worked for Terminalia Travel, which had only the vaguest interest in travel around the country, or around *this* world.

Terminalia Travel and everyone who worked there concerned themselves with the prospect of eventual travel around the multiverse. A prospect Andre had never even suspected was drawing closer to reality before Kelly and Marlene became part of his and Dana's lives.

As was always the case, even though he recognized Kelly's sweet little silver e-car as it parked behind his in front of Dana's house, Andre had no idea what the driver would look like until they stepped out.

Tonight *Miss* Kelly was behind the wheel, and she greeted Andre with a big grin and a bigger hug. Same wavy auburn hair and big, gorgeous hazel green eyes as ever, and she wore her typical near-uniform of khaki pants and a blue button-up shirt.

But tonight Kelly had a narrower jawline and shoulders, fuller lips, and softer skin that couldn't be explained away by clothing or makeup that she never wore.

Other changes besides a womanly chest and hips that all took place while Kelly slept completed the transformation from man to woman, and back again. Creating a double life that had only moved away from constantly stressful and even dangerous not all that long ago, when Kelly met the amazing woman who grabbed Andre in an even tighter hug.

Marlene stood a good bit shorter than either Kelly or Andre, and she definitely had curves in all the right places to go with long, wavy black hair and dimples to die for. She had a sassy style and flair Andre had admired from the start, from her big laugh to a spicy floral scent that he was beginning to suspect had nothing to do with perfume. Tonight's outfit featured a lacy pink blouse that fit tight around her considerable chest and waist before flaring out into a flirty half-skirt, all over narrow burgundy pants and glossy black shoes.

Anyone who saw the two of them together—no matter which gender Kelly had woken with that morning—understood in a heartbeat that they were a couple. And anyone who got to know them both understood why, from both sides of the equation.

"I am *so* glad to see you two," Andre said. "For the obvious reasons that you're both adorable, as usual. And because I get the strongest feeling I'm in over my head on the strangeness level here, and you *know* that's saying something."

Marlene stepped closer to Kelly, rotating her shoulders and tilting her head from side to side.

"I'm going to take a wild-ass guess that your strange thing is related to that *awful* chopping noise. How is anybody on this street managing to sleep right now? Or get through the day without screaming?"

Andre let out a gusty breath and sagged against his car, amazed at how a few words could leave him feeling weak and weightless at the same time.

"So you *do* hear it too. Thank all the gods of your choice and all the other ones waiting in line for their share of appreciation. I walked around the block last night to see how far it goes, and it's making a big, nerve-wracking circle in all directions. You getting anything at all, Kelly?"

Kelly turned her head from side to side, looking curious but not upset.

The thing that had drawn the four of them together in the first place was Marlene picking up the faint electronic signature of Andre's implant, and Andre picking up the unique dual sound Kelly made simply by existing in the world.

Marlene never did anything as amazing as going to sleep as a woman and waking up a man, and vice versa. Or any of the other talents and skills people drawn to Atlanta—and the multiverse anchored there—had as part of their everyday lives.

What Marlene had, besides a fantastic personality to go with her fashion sense, was the ability to hear another person like Kelly. Someone who thought they were a freak or a weirdo, that they'd never belong anywhere in the world and would be better off keeping themselves secret and hidden away.

Until they followed the undeniable pull to find their way to Atlanta, and discovered a home they never could have imagined.

"I don't hear a thing, no," Kelly said, reaching for Marlene's hand. "You said it sounds like *chopping*?"

"It does tonight, yeah." Andre waved one hand toward the east, where the noise got stronger. "It was churning the first night, like a fan out of balance, maybe. But it's gotten more and more...discordant, I think. Definitely more out of balance to my bionic ear. Like it's about to get itself organized enough to get it over with and break down altogether."

Marlene scowled and shook her head.

"Something may be breaking *through* instead of breaking down. Or about to, anyway." She shook her head and looked up at Dana's house, up on its little rise with only a faint light in one window. "Do we need to see to those sweet kitties before we do anything else? The last thing I'd ever want to do is deprive Jimi and Fizgig of their rightfully deserved spoiling."

"I loaded them up before you got here," Andre said. "So the ungrateful little beasties wouldn't go telling tales to Dana that I ignore them. That would only get back to my man Henry, who'd spread it on to Daisy Girl, then *she'd* be mad at me. Which I could not possibly tolerate."

He shrugged and smiled. "Dana did say we're all welcome to go inside, though, in case we need to...I don't know, whatever you do after looking into whatever's going on out here."

"We might take you up on that," Kelly said, "no matter how it goes. I'm always up for a good round of kitty spoiling. I don't think we'd get into anything too difficult tonight, but this is way more Marlene's area of expertise than mine. Hell, both of you have me beat when it comes to the extra senses."

"We're just extra sensible," Marlene said, leaning up to kiss Kelly's cheek. "But you might catch up if you hang around us enough. You never heard anything like this here before, Andre?"

"Not a trace," he said, shaking his head. "I last dropped by a few days before Dana left, but it was during the day. I don't know if it's louder at night, or if I just pick it up more because everything else is more quiet. Either way, it's new."

Marlene stared down the street for several seconds, rotating her shoulders again.

"Anything else strange? Or since we both already hear it, do you just want me to see how it affects me and we'll compare notes?"

Kelly raised her chin then, and Andre got the clear sense that she'd prefer a heck of a lot more information before Marlene went charging into the unknown.

"Hang on, I don't want either one of you to get hurt or walk into some kind of trouble I can't get you out of. Is it more than the noise, Andre?"

Andre looked into Marlene's eyes, consciously deferring to their shared enhanced senses. And Marlene's often-demonstrated sensibility when it came to matters of the multiverse.

After all, she'd been seeking out and welcoming new arrivals to Atlanta for years before Kelly crossed her path and won her heart.

"I think I'd like to see what happens," Marlene said, nodding at Andre before turning to face Kelly. "If it was dangerous, someone who lives here would have noticed, you know? If it's anything like our neighborhood, which it definitely is, people are out walking all day long. And Andre's just as fit and fine as ever."

Andre laughed despite his unusual case of skittery nerves and shivery hands.

"So kind of you to say so, my dear Marlene, especially since you're the next-best thing to divine yourself. I marked out where I noticed the effect, assuming my favorite beaded e-car is parked in about the same spot and no one's mowed down the daffodils. How about we all walk that way? That will let us know if whatever's happening is bigger or smaller, too."

Kelly breathed deep and blew out slowly. With her faint scowl and pursed lips, she looked like a perfect balance between her male and female selves.

"Okay, we'll try it. Probably best to know if I notice anything at all beside you two specially endowed sleuths."

Kelly suffered a quick joint hug from both Andre and Marlene with a snort and a smile. Then Marlene stepped in between and grabbed both their hands.

"I suppose we should all take turns once we get there," she said. "But let's walk together."

Before Andre was quite ready, he pulled them to a stop between the daffodils and the e-car, which had acquired a thick strand of sparkly lime-green beads around the passenger headrest sometime during the day. The chopping noise took on a worrisome grinding note tonight, one he didn't want to get closer to.

What surprised him was how much he didn't want Marlene or Kelly to get close either, even though several houses had to be within the huge circular zone he'd walked the night before.

"Doesn't seem bigger than last night," he said, "at least not in this direction."

"But you said the sound is getting worse," Kelly said. "So we need to be careful, which I'm sure you both already know."

"We do, sweetie." Marlene squeezed Andre's hand and reached across to grasp Kelly's for a second, then stood alone. "And I trust both of you to yank me right back if you need to."

Without so much as a kiss or a wink or a glance backward, Marlene stepped forward.

One step.

Two, then three.

And she stopped, unmoving long enough to send Andre's heart pounding, and grabbing for Kelly's hand. She squeezed back.

"That's long enough for me," Kelly said, but

before she more than leaned forward, Marlene turned to face them.

Even in the faint light, the surprise on her face was clear, as was her mouthing a silent "wow" before she walked back.

"That's not at *all* what I expected," she said, breathless and wide-eyed. "But I'm not going to say anything until you try it, Kelly. We should test the extra-sensory thing for sure before... Anyway, we should test it."

Kelly raised her eyebrows and blinked, then held out both hands to the side.

"Now y'all got me curious," she said, and stepped toward the invisible line.

The same three steps forward, with both Andre and Marlene holding their breath.

But instead of stopping cold, Kelly slowed, moving several more feet before she put her hands on her hips and came to a standstill. Andre saw her look to the left and right before she slowly turned and walked back, shaking her head the whole time.

Kelly's dazed expression and relieved sigh told a whole lot of the story before she opened her mouth.

"Okay, that was...bizarre. I'll go first since I was last in there. The air got almost sludgy around me, even more than a muggy, hot day with bucketloads of pollen. I was sure I'd need to run up to Dana's and jump in the shower, but that grubby feeling disappeared as soon as I stepped back out. Your turn."

Andre and Kelly turned to Marlene, who held her head to once side and looked a question at Kelly.

"Did you hear anything in there? Or *not* hear anything?"

Kelly shrugged. "Everything sounded kind of muted, like my ears needed to pop, you know? But I didn't hear anything like what you two are describing. You?"

"I could hear about the same as you," Marlene said. "And the air did feel gummy like you said. But I felt like part of me got turned off. Probably the part that can hear when I'm close to someone different, like you, Kelly. That noise faded down to almost nothing in there, but it never went away. Still sounded awful though, like something is about to let go."

Chills ran along Andre's arms and legs despite the warm night.

"Something about to let go is the best way I've heard it yet," he said. "When I went in there last night and again before you got here, my processor cut out completely. Nothing besides a big damn magnet or an extremely illegal cell phone jammer should be able to do that. My phone worked just fine, never even dropped the call with Dana. I didn't think about the air being too thick, but that explains why I felt like the breeze never touched me."

Marlene looked at each of them, then turned toward the weirdness zone.

"So I think we're onto something, and I haven't the faintest idea what it could be. But it doesn't feel *dangerous* to me. What I think we should do is ping someone we trust to let them know what we're doing, then go in and see what we can find. Or better, maybe I go and Andre goes, but you stay out here, Kelly."

Kelly scowled again and started to speak, but Marlene touched her cheek.

"I know, you don't have to say it, but hear me out. *You're* the someone I trust most. And you know who to call if this gets weirder than it already is. I'd go by myself, but I'd feel better with someone else along. Someone else who can hear this thing. Anyway, Andre found it, so I say he gets to go if he wants to."

This time Kelly frowned, but she didn't shake her head. Andre wondered for a hot second how *Mr.* Kelly would react with the additional testosterone coursing through his veins.

"Has anyone ever found anything dangerous here?" Kelly said. "Related to the multiverse, I mean? I know things are ramping up, but I've never heard of a big zone of *noise* like this. Not that I can hear this one."

"No, nothing dangerous," Marlene said. "Not yet. One danger we have been looking out for is some kind of passage opening up. An uncontrolled connection between one side and the other. We've only had one person come through to our side so far, out in Little Five."

She turned to Andre. "Mr. Thomas, our first interdimensional liaison."

As if one single word of what she'd said should have rung any kind of bell inside Andre's head besides the "what in blazes have I missed or misunderstood now" bell, she went on.

"You remember Mr. Thomas was a couple of days early, Kelly, but we were expecting him. No one's expecting whatever is happening here."

"So maybe we wait and bring in more people," Kelly said, crossing her arms. "Backups other than me."

"Wait, I heard Marlene say *not yet* just then," Andre said. "Don't think I missed that little bit of information slipped in there all innocent. Thing is, whatever's going on isn't sounding smoother or calmer or anything cheerful like that. It's sounding rougher. About to break down or break through."

Andre stood straight and tall, head up and eyes wide open, same as he had over and over again all the years of his life.

Conjuring up confidence even when he was afraid.

Stepping out fierce despite his fears, large or small.

"I say we get in there and check it out," he said, "before it really does get worse. If your backup is anything like mine or Dana's, we'll all be waiting here a lot longer than any of us are comfortable with."

Marlene grinned and kissed Kelly quick on the lips.

"Okay, okay," Kelly said, with a smile that read more than a little bit resigned. "Do this much for me, if you could. It was a good idea to text someone, and we all three should do that. Then you start a call with me, both of you, so I can at least hear what's going on. Same way Dana heard you the other day, Andre."

A few quick seconds later, texts sent and conference call started, Andre and Marlene faced east.

"Let's get moving before my nerve starts to slip," Andre said, "or Dana calls to *strongly* encourage me to come to my unusual set of senses."

Marlene grabbed his hand, and they walked forward.

Barely three steps into a distressingly moist and skin-clinging silence that looked so strangely like a typical old East Atlanta neighborhood.

Andre turned to Marlene and pointed to his left

ear. She shook her head. He let go of her hand and raised his phone to tap out a message, then rolled his eyes at his own damn foolishness.

He then spoke in an absurdly exaggerated fashion, the same way a handful of folks still did when they realized he'd been hearing impaired since birth.

He hoped he didn't look nearly as silly as they usually did before he pointed out the reality of his implant.

In this moment, he didn't mind one bit to trot out his oldest reliable skill for getting along in a hearing world: one that wasn't susceptible to interference, battery glitches, or any sort of previously unknown multidimensional phenomena.

"I can read lips. So don't be afraid to speak up."

Marlene nodded and raised her free hand in a thumbs up.

"I can barely hear it still. Want to keep going, see if it gets stronger?"

Andre nodded, and his phone buzzed in his hand. Dana, threatening him with severe bodily harm if his fool stubbornness got his body harmed. He held his phone up at the same time as Marlene.

Kelly's message was simpler, and Andre knew she was every bit as concerned as Dana. Just a bit more gentle about showing it.

Hear you loud and clear, and still no noise for me.

Backup on the way, agree you're the best ones for the job. Be right here.

Both Marlene and Andre blew kisses to Kelly on the other side of the invisible barrier.

Then they simply kept going.

Despite the seeming normality of everything he could see, Andre was startled when a car turned off the street ahead and drove toward them. He and Marlene stepped aside, looking back to make sure Kelly did the same.

The driver and passenger showed no signs of noticing the unearthly noise, or the silence.

"Backup?" Andre said.

Marlene shook her head. "Too soon. How far is the middle of the zone?"

Andre pointed past the street the car had come from, about two more houses past, then held up one hand and tilted it back and forth.

"Good enough," Marlene said. "Let me know if anything changes, and I'll do the same."

Their walk could have been an ordinary neighborhood stroll on a warm spring evening, extra-sticky air aside. Dark but with that orange city-glow overhead, not much moving in one of Atlanta's oldest residential communities. Passing houses dark or fully lit or somewhere in between, with every make and model of e-car crouched out front or snugged up in a short driveway.

But that feeling of something strange, something *off*, that hit Andre on the first night he'd noticed the freaky churning sound was back, and stronger than ever.

Still not threatening, at least not to him.

But too strong and peculiar to ignore.

When they reached the middle of the second block, he realized they'd both strayed toward the left side. In front of one of the wonderful empty spaces these original neighborhoods sometimes still held tight like a favorite—or most useful—secret bit of juicy gossip.

A patch of grass and trees and flowers, with raised garden beds around the edges, that managed to survive skyrocketing turn-of-the-millennium housing prices decades ago without a house wedged in.

Tonight, the coveted open ground didn't project the usual welcoming breath of fresh air, or chance for a bit of green-tinted peace and quiet.

Now an ethereal scarlet glow suffused the far edge of the grass, close enough to the opposite side of the block that Andre would have seen it when he walked past the night before.

Before he could say a word, even a word he couldn't hear, Marlene grabbed his arm.

"Was that there last night?" she said, her lip movements clear in the red-tinted light.

Andre shook his head.

"Feel scary to you?"

He shook his head again, because the little garden spot didn't feel the least bit scary. Only that deepening sense of eerie.

But that didn't stop him from jumping and nearly dropping his phone when it buzzed.

I know you're together there and all, but mind getting me an update? I'm stuck out here in the arctic tundra worrying about you!

He tapped out *All good, nothing to update yet. Queen Marlene and me getting close!* before he turned the phone toward the queen herself.

Marlene rolled her eyes, then turned and waved toward Kelly, who'd resumed her spot in the middle of the quiet street.

"We're fine, Kelly," she said into her own phone. "Going to check this out, only a few steps off the road." To Andre she said "I can hear the sound again now, but not quite as loud as outside. Calmer, too. It really does sound like one of our new arrivals."

Andre pointed to his ear and shook his head, but he lifted his phone again. He switched to his implant app and adjusted the input levels down to what he couldn't help thinking of as Dana level.

He shook his head again, pointed to his implant, then Marlene's ear. Maybe this was one time his bionic sense fell a little bit short of the uncanny gift she'd been born with.

They held hands again and stepped onto the softer grass of the pocket-sized park.

Despite the continuing refusal of his processor to do the one and only job it had to do, Andre knew some kind of sound came from the scarlet glow they walked toward. He felt it through the sluggish air, in his bones, even in his teeth.

A low, thrumming pulse that he knew matched the chopping he'd heard before.

Ahead of them, the glow deepened and grew more intense, somehow getting brighter and darker at the same time.

Then it concentrated right behind one of the low-sided wooden garden boxes still empty so early in springtime.

The light took on the same pulsating cycle of the air itself, matching the noise Andre couldn't hear.

When he and Marlene stood only a few feet away, the light drew itself back into one throbbing point.

And it *grew*, rising up away from the ground in a few heart-stopping seconds.

Andre resisted the screaming demands from his belly and heart and brain and everywhere else, to drag himself and Marlene the hell away from whatever was about to go down right in front of them.

But she only stood there, watching the shape shift and grow until it stood taller than Andre.

Taller than anyone he'd ever met or imagined outside of a fantasy movie, too long and too thing to possibly stand upright.

Soft, stubby forms jutted out from the top and sides, forming into a head and arms that were also longer than anything outside one of the surrealist paintings Andre's man Henry loved so much.

The limbs stretched out and the whole shape *flexed*, bulging out and bright/dark red enough to make Andre's eyes water.

And still, Marlene never moved.

She finally held out both hands with her palms up and smiled.

The pulsating ripples through Andre's mind and body stopped.

He recognized Marlene's one quiet word.

"Welcome."

The shape thickened with one final thump more felt than heard.

And all the normal sounds returned to the night.

Most clearly of all, Andre's near-panicked breathing.

His skin still felt clammy, but he realized it was from his own sweat rather than air grabbing too much of a hold to be natural, even in the South.

He leaned toward Marlene, not taking his eyes

away from the form that resembled a human more by the second.

Quite lovely if he was being honest with himself, or at least it would be once his pulse dropped somewhere below the range of don't-even-ask-just-sit-your-ass-down-and-breathe.

He was looking at an altogether gorgeous creature of some kind, if you ignored the baking scarlet glow.

"Did you just say '*welcome*'?" he whispered.

"Of *course* I did," Marlene whispered right back. "What did your mamma teach *you* say when you meet someone new? Especially a trans-dimensional liaison?"

Andre drew breath to speak louder and defend his own Proper Southern Boy manners, not to mention his mamma's well-deserved reputation and honor.

Never mind that he proceeded to lose his considerable grasp of the English language as the shape formed a creepily narrow version of a head and aimed a pair of glowing eyes toward them.

Eyes that glittered electric green and whirled in every direction, with no reason or rhyme he could detect.

It was probably a blessing all around that whatever they were standing in front of figured out how to get ahold of words before Andre did. Even if the words bypassed his processor altogether and landed neatly inside his quivering jellified mass of a brain.

"I am sorry for this intrusion, without warning or invitation. We did not intend to appear in this place. So very far from our agreed-upon communication point."

Thankfully Marlene spoke out loud, sparing Andre the embarrassing potential of curling up in a ball and willing himself to faint if she'd planted words inside his head.

"You're not far, not considering the breadth and depth of your travels to reach us here. Only a few of our miles away. Would you like us to take you there?"

"My purpose does not require full dimensional transfer. I bring news and a warning that will affect our interdimensional travel for a short time. Our first liaison arrived here in an unexpected manner."

Marlene nodded, and Andre scratched and clawed his mind back into motion.

"Mr. Thomas," he said. "The one who showed up early out in Little Five."

Marlene smiled and patted his shoulder, like he'd just managed to tie his shoe properly for the first time after days of trying.

She wasn't far off from the way he felt.

"We have determined our first liaison's troubled arrival was due to a miscalculation in

OUR TRANS-DIMENSIONAL MATRIX. ONE THAT HAS CONTINUED TO DETERIORATE IN A DANGEROUS MANNER. THAT IS WHY I WAS UNABLE TO COMMUNICATE IN THE AGREED-UPON WAY. I MUST ALSO APOLOGIZE FOR MY UNFORGIVABLE DELAY IN WARNING YOU OF THIS PROBLEM, AND THANK YOU FOR ARRIVING WHEN YOU DID. MY INTRUSION INTO YOUR WORLD WOULD NOT HAVE LASTED ONE MORE CYCLE OF YOUR ORBITAL STAR."

"Delay..." Marlene paused, then gasped and turned to Andre, grabbing both of his arms. "You know what this means? You saved us, maybe *all* of us."

"I'm entirely relieved and glad to help, as always," Andre said, "but honey, you're going to have to back up all the way to Nashville before I have the slightest idea what you're talking about."

Marlene laughed and pulled him into a quick hug, then turned back to the creature Andre truly wished he could get a picture of for Henry.

But he was too scared for his phone and for himself to try.

"Thank you, Liaison," Marlene said, "for your considerable energy and effort in warning us. We'll delay our next operations until we hear from you again. Do you think you can return to this same location?"

"WOULD THIS BE SAFER THAN ATTEMPTING TO

REACH OUR NORMAL COMMUNICATION POINT? IF SO, WE CAN RETURN HERE."

"This would be the best target," Marlene said. "Until we work together to refine the problem in our matrix, this would be the safest. We know to watch for you now. Please take your leave when you're ready rather than expending so much energy, and we look forward to our next contact with you."

The creature amped up that light/dark glow again, and Andre forced himself not to cover his eyes with his hands.

That couldn't possibly be a polite way to respond to his first interdimensional liaison.

"WE THANK YOU BOTH. AND WE TOO LOOK FORWARD TO OUR NEXT CONTACT."

The liaison bent forward in an unmistakable bow, and Andre and Marlene did the same.

A crimson burst of lightning strobed the night away.

And it was gone.

The spring night settled warm and soft around them.

Time, and space, and at least one dimension, returned to normal.

Andre barely yanked back a most ungentlemanly scream at a voice from right behind him.

"Wow," Kelly said. "No wonder you two heard something strange."

Marlene hugged Kelly, then Andre, giggling the whole time.

"Did you hear that, Kelly? Without Andre, we could have had a serious nightmare on our hands."

This time Kelly nearly squeezed out all the air Andre finally dragged back into his lungs.

"She's not kidding, Andre. You just might have saved us all."

"Well, you must know I certainly am glad to hear that, but I'm still wondering what I did, exactly. Or should I hold off on that until I have a full-night's sleep or possibly an extra-strong cocktail?"

Kelly raised her eyebrows and smiled.

"Don't worry, you're not losing your grasp on anything, except maybe your phone. Let's call off the backup that may very well have showed up too late, go back to Dana's place, cuddle the kitties into oblivion, and get her on speakerphone if you think she's still awake. I have no doubt she'll want to hear all about this herself."

Andre scowled, only then noticing he didn't have anything in his hand, or in his pocket. He finally spotted it by the glow and buzz of an incoming text message.

"Dana's *very* much awake," he said, picking it up. "And about to blow one of her nerdy little gaskets, since I apparently missed a great multitude of rather pointed inquiries from her. I just wish Henry wasn't on these damn nighttime photoshoots so he could listen in."

Marlene slipped her arm around Kelly.

"We'll be more than happy to fill him in when he gets back. You might be surprised at how well you'll be able to do it yourself once we walk you through the entry-level overview of the risks and rewards of building and maintaining an interdimensional matrix."

"And the potential dangers of trying to use one you didn't realize was deteriorating," Kelly chimed in. "If you hadn't paid attention and called us when you did, a hell of a lot more than our communications might have gotten tangled up in a mess. The city, state, and possibly the whole southeast should be thanking you, really."

They started walking, and Andre forced his wobbly legs to get it together and follow.

"You two know enough about this whole matrix thing to explain it to me?"

"We can cover the basics for sure," Marlene said with a wink. "Once you're ready for more, we can get you in front of the geniuses who make it go. The ones on our side, at least for now."

Andre drew breath to ask something else, then stopped and laughed at himself. He and Dana had known these two for a while, and they'd heard a good bit about the work they were doing. But he wouldn't even pretend to know enough about the way it all worked to ask sensible questions.

After the last few days and especially the last hour or so, he was plenty damn eager and ready to learn.

"I'll hold off on the experts for now," he said, catching up with Marlene and Kelly. "But kitty cuddles and spoiling are definitely in order. Let me call Dana right now before she reaches right through this phone and snatches me bald-headed, which truly would be a shame."

She picked up on the first ring.

"*Andre!* Where the hell have you—"

"Just hold on, Dana my dear. We're heading back to your place, where Kelly and Marlene will do their best to explain what happened here, and why you'll wish even more that you never left home in the first place. All I'll say is I'm sorry for making you wait. And you're not going to *believe* what just moved into your sweet little neighborhood."

KARI KILGORE

AUTHOR OF ODDS AND ENDINGS AND THE EARWORMS

Sunny with a Chance of Happiness

A Lightning Gap Story

For every four-legged soul who rescues me

SUNNY WITH A
CHANCE OF HAPPINESS

GEORGE EDWARDS WONDERED what evil twist of nature made kids magically transform themselves into adults right around the time their parents realized they were middle-aged. Simple biology and math couldn't possibly explain such cruelty.

Or maybe it was just him not stopping to look around him often enough, just like his little sister Sophie always said.

Either way, he very much wanted to file a complaint. Ask for a do-over.

Convince his own sweet twins to come back and hang out with the old man just a little bit longer.

George sat on his broad front porch thinking his gloomy, aged thoughts, doing his best to ignore the spectacular sunrise unfolding all around him. Not at all conducive for a good bout of feeling sorry for himself.

The house perched on the outskirts of Lightning Gap, Virginia, right on the edge between the national forest that covered the mountain and the town tucked away at the top. The sky overhead had barely shifted from pink to the faintest blue, without a cloud to break up the wash of color.

If he walked out into the yard and turned to the right, he'd catch sight of the town's namesake and most distinctive feature: the sheltering limestone ridge that cradled Lightning Gap, ending with the towering spike of the Lightning Stone itself. Target of the unusual number of electrical storms that passed through. He'd spent part of the long night before enjoying a brash, particularly noisy one passing through, with gales of rain, brilliant flashes of lightning, and thunder to rattle the windows.

George knew he wasn't the only one that at least half-believed that stone and the storms were the source of the town's peculiar magic.

The valley seemed to ripple below him as the last of the morning mist burned off, and the illusion of water continued in the contours of the land. One ridge after the other, each one covered with thick stands of hickory, oak, maple, and pine trees. From here, he could see what looked like all of Felten

County gradually lighting up in a thousand shades of deep late-summer green.

All of them cloaked in full September splendor.

George listened to his stomach gurgle contentedly, working down what his son Tommy and his daughter Trina would have considered an unusually healthy breakfast for him. Two scrambled eggs, whole wheat toast with just enough butter to taste, a whole luscious red garden tomato sliced up over the whole thing.

He'd even listened to Sophie's sisterly advice to switch from regular brewed coffee to cold brew, to cut down on the acid first thing in the morning.

He hadn't admitted how much smoother it tasted.

From where he'd settled on the porch steps, George could kick his bare feet through the dew-damp grass, stirring up the wonderful scent of freshly cut green. Just chilly enough to be refreshing with weeks of hot weather still to come. His brown steel-toed work boots sat beside him, black socks folded on top, ready to join up with his jeans, t-shirt, leather gloves, and faded blue baseball cap for a busy day.

Even though he wanted nothing more than to hang around his unreasonably empty house and mope, trees all around Lightning Gap and Felten County had the bad manners to keep falling. Especially after a storm blew through. Which meant

George had to pull himself together before he joined Sophie in their tree-clearing business.

The only one more likely to tell George to buck up and keep going than Sophie was their father.

He kicked his feet again, letting his own memories of fatherhood wash up like the dew.

Trina on this porch, standing barely three feet high, hands on her little hips. Loudly demanding that Tommy *stop* whatever annoying thing he was doing *right that very minute.*

Tommy ignoring her with an irresistible grin, his black curls matching Trina's, and George's before silver started creeping in around the edges.

Trina much taller, pushing the same mower George had pushed yesterday. Tommy running the weedeater. Both of them convinced they'd been stuck with the worst part of the job. Never mind that they'd both still think that when they traded machines the next time.

Their mother Lacy, the most beautiful woman in the whole world from the second George saw her in college down in Hidden Springs. Even more so when she carried those two perfect babies, and for the first three years of their lives.

On the porch swing with their tiny brand-new humans, holding them both and staring at George beside her, eyes full of wonder. Laughing and wiping away tears as they toddled away from her for the first time across the grass.

Before she was carried away from all of them on a tide made of bad news from one doctor after another, then hospital rooms, and last breaths George could still feel against his cheek.

"Wish you were here, Gracie. They both started college last week. Not down in Hidden Springs where I first caught sight of you, but one off in Atlanta and the other out in Nashville. They send me pictures from their phones just about every day, but I miss them more than I could admit to anyone but you. You'd be *so* proud, sweetheart. I know I am."

George took a deep, nostalgia-laced breath, reached for his socks, and froze.

A rustling noise erupted from the trees and brush to his right.

Too big to be a squirrel.

Not big enough to be a bear, *right*? Anyway, black bears weren't likely to be too aggressive this time of year. No brand-new cubs to keep an eye on like back in the early spring.

Still, George strained to listen and see, ready to head for the front door in a hurry. He'd heard the rumors about mountain lions still hanging on in an area they were supposedly extinct from.

Heard more than a few of those bone-chilling screams in the night, too.

When the brush finally parted, he let out a grunt and relaxed a little.

Not a bear or any sort of cat after all.

A dog burst out into the yard instead.

A good-sized white dog with several big black spots, probably close to fifty pounds. Short hair, floppy triangular ears, one black and one white. Kind of a wide, blocky head matched with the slender build of a pointer.

Huge brown eyes looking all around the yard before focusing on George with a laser-like intensity.

Then a wide, happy grin, with an altogether-too-long pink tongue lolling out the side of its mouth.

"Well hey there. Where'd you come from? Get separated from your people out on the trails?"

George wouldn't recommend going cross-country from his place to the sprawling network of trails in and around Lightning Gap. Too many dense thickets of rhododendrons, which were accurately called hells.

But the dog had come from that direction.

The dog who took several steps until it...no, *she*...was only about ten feet away. She sat and panted at him, still with that big goofy smile.

"Can't say I see a collar on you, either. I doubt you'd be grinning that big if you had designs on taking a chomp out of me, huh? Come on over here and let's see."

George whistled low rising to high, the same way he'd heard his parents and other people with dogs do. Same as he'd done with a long series of sweet pups during his own childhood, before he married Lacy with her truly awful allergies to dogs and cats and most other critters with hair.

The dog in his yard perked up her ears and tilted her head to one side, but she didn't come any closer.

"I'm not going to hurt you, girl. Promise. Haven't had a dog for longer than I care to admit, but I remember more or less how it's done. Let me get you into town and see if anyone's looking for you. Pretty thing like you, I bet someone's missing you awful."

He tried to stop the thought, but it barged into his mind anyway.

Same way I miss my kids. And my wife.

And any kind of normal, happy routine at home that keeps me out of the achy, empty spaces in my mind and my heart.

The dog stood, shaking herself all over, starting with sharp popping sounds her ears and ending with an energetic wiggle of her tail. George was surprise to see drops of water fly off in a spray all around her.

"What on earth have you been into?" He clicked his tongue against the roof of his mouth, and laughed when she tilted her head the other way. "I hope you weren't out in that big storm all night long. Still grinning at me at least. Listen, I bet you'd like a piece of cheese or bread or something. Then I'll get you into town and see if we can't find your people."

He got to his feet slowly, holding both hands down so he wouldn't look like he was going to try to grab her. She simply watched him, showing no signs of distress or fear.

"Think you can stay put for a minute or two? Don't run again, now. I'd hate for you to end up on the road with someone not paying attention to what's in front of them."

The dog stared for another few seconds, then abruptly closed her mouth with a faint snap. She walked toward him slowly, still watching. Her head and ears were up, not cowered under. Her tail was low, but it waved back and forth.

George was pretty sure he recognized the language even after years away from having dogs of his own. He and Sophie had met more than enough four-legged guardians in the process of removing trees, either before or after they'd crashed them-selves to the ground.

Some were furious at the intrusion, most often barking their fool heads off from behind their people. Some were joyful and welcoming, as if George's visit was only a reunion that had been delayed for far too long.

But a few had the same look as this dog. Not angry, not overly confident.

More...hopeful. He could just about see a furry little black and white thought bubble above her head.

Please be a nice person.

Please don't hurt me.

George squatted slowly, relieved when his knees didn't go off like firecrackers. He turned his face down and to the side like his parents taught him when meeting a strange dog for the first time. Same way he'd taught his twins.

A direct stare could seem like a threat, and remember, a human smiling might not look all that different from a dog baring its teeth.

Give them the best chance to do the right thing that you possibly can.

He almost snorted, not sure if his thoughts were better for his long-ago attempts at dating after Lacy, or more like the running monologue he kept with himself when faced with red-faced or sullen children.

The dog was only a few feet away now, and still cautiously wagging her tail.

George held out his right hand, fingers curled under.

"It's okay, girl," he said in a quiet voice. "I know how hard it is to meet someone new. Especially when you're feeling lost and lonely."

He felt warm breath across his knuckles, a series

of quick sniffs, then a big blow out. Another sniff, then a couple of quick licks. What his mother always called kissies.

George rubbed the back of his hand along the wet fur of the dog's cheek, and she leaned into his touch. When he glanced up, her tail was high and wagging madly.

"Okay then. Maybe you might decide to trust me after all."

She stepped forward and pushed the top of her head against his leg, almost like a cat. Instead of the sulfurous reek of skunk he'd been half-afraid of, she smelled like she'd run through a creek or stream. Sort of mossy, with the typical wet-dog aroma underneath.

She didn't feel grubby or oily or muddy either. Only wet.

Not at all like a dog who'd been on her own for very long.

When he scratched behind her ears and along her back, her tail picked up momentum until her whole backside swayed along with it.

"Now we're making progress. I'm going to scoot back onto the porch before I stand up, how's that sound?"

When he did, she followed along with him, walking herself from one side to the other, then back, leaning into his hands. He had the strangest feeling she was trying to show him how to pet her, as if she'd decided he just didn't know how.

George obliged until she either had enough or decided he was a hopeless case. She turned around and sat with her rump on his bare feet, letting out a contented sigh big enough that her lips flapped. The warm and damp pressure on his toes was somehow almost as pleasant as the grass had been earlier.

He scratched the extra-thick hair on her neck, not feeling a trace of a flattened spot where a collar might have been.

When he stood, she jumped up and took a couple of steps, but showed no signs of fear or getting ready to bolt. In fact, when he walked up the steps, she got so close behind that her head bumped against his thighs.

"No, you can't go inside. Sorry about that. It's just that..."

He closed his eyes and his mouth, surprised and yet resigned to what he'd been about to say. His kids had never shown any signs of inheriting Lacy's allergies. But he'd held onto that worry for some unlikely reason he couldn't even remember now.

"Anyway, it's best if you stay out here for a minute. I just want to grab that cheese for you, and maybe something to use as a leash. Then we'll head into town."

She sat again, her tail brushing back and forth

over the brown-painted wood of the porch. Still with that happy, relaxed canine grin that had George smiling whether he wanted to or not.

He nodded once, opened the screen door, and stepped inside.

He was even more surprised at how much he hoped she was still out there when he returned.

Slices of regular old American cheese retrieved—and broken up into smaller squares so she wouldn't try to gobble it all at once and get choked—and with a length of light sisal rope tossed over his shoulder, George paused just inside the door.

A contented sigh nearly as big as the dog's just a few minutes before escaped him, and a bloom of warmth from deep in his heart surged through him.

The black and white dog had curled herself up on the porch, pressed so close against the screen door that he saw bits of her fur poking through. From her soft and even breathing, he got a pretty good idea she'd fallen asleep.

So fast.

And so *trusting*, of someone she'd only met less than ten minutes ago.

Someone would be heartbroken over this girl wandering off and getting lost for sure. Much as he hated to wake her, George didn't want her or her people to wait longer than they had to.

As soon as he took one more step, she stretched,

pushing all four legs straight out and leaning her neck back. Then she rolled gracefully onto her feet, pressed her nose against the screen, and breathed in with that rapid-fire sniffing.

"Yeah, it's me. Told you I'd be right back."

She backed up and resumed her wagging-so-hard-I'm-swaying routine with the sweet grin close behind.

George stepped through the screen door, pulling the wooden door closed behind him. Time to get moving if he was going to ask around before meeting Sophie at their dad's shop.

It didn't matter that their father hadn't been coming in more than a couple of times a week lately. The cavernous garage packed full of the tools for cutting huge trees, the tools to maintain those tools, and the tools to maintain the huge, crotchety truck parked inside would always be the old man's domain.

The dog happily took a couple of the cheese squares, and didn't seem to care one bit when George looped the rope around her neck. The next square got the rope adjusted with a knot to keep it from pulling too tight.

He sat to put on his shoes and socks, and she pushed her nose in between his arm and ribs. Laughing, he popped another couple of squares into her mouth. She let him get one shoe tied before she switched to the other side and accepted the reward of the last bits of cheese.

"I'm fresh out now," he said, holding up both hands. She sniffed each one, then sneezed. "I'll get you some real food while we're out in town. I mean, I'll get a bag to go with you. When you go back home, I hope."

George leaned forward and concentrated on pulling thick laces through the boot's metal loops, wondering why he felt guilty and sneaky in equal measures. This poor sweet stray had no reason to expect to stay here with him. And he certainly wouldn't be willing to take someone's beloved pet without at least trying to find her family.

He decided not to think about when he *would* be willing to take this dog in.

Going down that path seemed like a sure way to end up even more sad and lonely than he'd been before she came crashing out of the woods.

He stood, looped the end of the rope around his hand, and clicked his tongue again. When she grinned up at him, he took several pictures with his phone, figuring he could send them to anyone who might have word of a lost dog.

"All right, pretty girl. Let's head on out."

She walked at his right side without hesitation, only pulling a tiny bit at the rope.

Yeah, this one would definitely be going back home with someone soon.

And no doubt they'd be overjoyed to get those sweet kissies.

GEORGE ONLY MADE it a couple of miles toward Lightning Gap before his phone started the usual buzzing-like-crazy routine in his pocket. The clear boundary between rotten signal at his house and picking up the tower in town.

He'd endured more than enough safety lectures from both Tommy and Trina to even consider getting it out to check the messages.

Little did they know what kind of craziness he'd gotten up to during his own growing-up years around here. Of course that thought led directly to how glad *he* was to not know too much about what they'd gotten up to themselves.

He glanced at the dog sitting tall and proud in the passenger seat of his truck, keeping an eye on the trees passing by, perking her ears up every time a vehicle went by in the opposite direction. His silver Chevy wasn't one of those silly jacked-up models you had to climb into, or anywhere near as tall as his dad's big work truck. Not the cushy version, either, more sedan than pickup, with delicate seats that had a dozen adjustments and nowhere near the sturdy upholstery the job demanded.

Still, he'd half-expected to need to help the dog up. But she'd jumped into the floorboard, then right up into the seat to face forward, like she'd been in that exact same spot the day before.

When he got to a fairly straight stretch of Lightning Rock Road, George tapped the dash display. Sure enough, a text message from Sophie popped up first thing. Partly because he didn't love the idea of getting himself into a wreck over the pure foolishness of trying to read a message, and partly because he knew it bugged her, he tapped the phone icon beside her name.

Only one ring sounded through the truck's speakers, getting the dog's increasingly adorable head-tilt, before Sophie answered.

"You just *have* to call me, don't you?"

"Would you rather have me driving distracted, Sis? What would your niece and nephew think? Or our father?"

"They'd all think you call more to annoy me than anything else. Where are you?"

"Heading that way, just outside the town limits. I need to make a quick stop first. Busy day on the books?"

"Not especially, calmer than usual after a big overnight rumble. Might be a good time to get all the tools and this grouchy old truck cleaned and serviced while we can. Are you stopping by Kay's Café for coffee or breakfast? Because I wouldn't mind one bit if you brought in extra."

"I made my own breakfast, thank you very much. One my fussy kids would actually approve of. I've got kind of a lost soul who showed up at my place, trying to get her back to her people."

The line went silent, but George could see the call was still connected. He played his words back in his mind and rolled his eyes. He'd given her a tremendous opening. Sophie would be sitting back if she was sitting down, with a combination scowl/frown that she wouldn't try to hide even if he was right in front of her.

"Should I even ask who this lost soul is, or what she wants? Or why she went to your place to begin with?"

"You can ask all those questions, sure. And all she'll be able to do is grin and lick your hand, assuming she likes you as much as she seems to like me."

Sophie snorted into the phone, and George heard the smile in her voice.

"I'm going to assume you're talking about a dog rather than a cat, right? What happened, she just showed up?"

George slowed to a stop beside the big, modern

hardware store just outside of Lightning Gap, waiting for what seemed like a parade of cars to turn in from both directions. He took the opportunity to rub the dog's head. She leaned hard into his hand, tongue lolling out what looked like a foot.

"She walked right out of the woods while I was sitting on the porch. Friendly little thing, too. Listen, do you know if there's any kind of...I don't know, a lost and found for the trails around town, or the forest service? Someone I can report a missing dog to?"

"I don't know of anything, no. Nothing official, anyway. There's the vet in town, Dr. Robinette. She's an absolute sweetheart with our critters."

Sophie and her mutually-head-over-heels boyfriend Craig had taken in a pair each of stray dogs and cats who showed up around the same time they moved in together, and George had to admit they were delightful creatures. His kids loved spending time around them, too.

"Dr. Robinette's office is a couple of houses down from Odds and Endings, right?"

Even over the phone, he caught the strange sound of Sophie's laugh. As if she had a secret about the wonderful bookstore that really was the heart and soul of Lightning Gap, or at least knew something he wasn't quite catching on to. He drove on past the vast parking lot in front of the new hardware store, thankful he wouldn't have to get into that big crowd.

"Dr. Robinette is just past Odds and Endings, yeah," she said. "You might even be better off stopping in there first, since they're open and the vet won't be until nine. I doubt there's much the Seagons don't know about before anyone else in town. If someone is missing a good dog, that would be a great place to start."

George followed the last curve and their lovely hometown came into view. The long, straight road in front of him was full of stately Victorian houses painted a spectacular variety of colors, with the vibrant purple turret room on top of Odds and Endings the tallest of the bunch. A row of cute shops beyond that, then the solid red brick of the high school he and Sophie and his twins had all graduated from across the far end.

And beyond *that*, the massive limestone ridge that sheltered Lightning Gap, and the exclamation point of the Lightning Stone to the left.

"What's on your mind, Sophie? Sounds like you're trying to get me to do something I'll regret."

She responded with a theatrical gasp, and the dog beside George whipped her head around so fast her ears flapped.

"How *could* you accuse me of such a thing? And me your very own dear sister."

George passed the first several Victorians, then slowed when he got close to Odds and Endings. As almost always seemed to happen when he wanted to drop by, even in such a small town without much parking, a spot was open right in front. That never failed to surprise him, especially right across the street from the breakfast-crowd-busy Kay's Café tucked into the ground floor of another lovely old Victorian.

"I'm not accusing you of anything," he said. "I've just known you since you were born is all. Maybe I'll stop in here and see, then walk my guest here on down to the vet. I haven't stopped in at Odds and Endings for longer than I want to admit."

He pulled into the spot and leaned over, amused at how the dog peered up at the bookstore the same way he did. The purple was accented with green and blue on the elaborate woodwork, and chairs all over the broad porch out front were outfitted with matching cushions.

"That's exactly what you should do," Sophie said. "Don't worry, I'm sure Craig and I can dig up some spare doggie stuff if you need it. Talk to you later."

She ended the call before George could answer, leaving him shaking his head as he often did when he knew—he *knew*—she was keeping something from him.

"Nothing to do for it, girl," he said, scratching the

dog's head and neck thoroughly. "I've been trying since the day they brought her home from the hospital, and she always gets the better of me. Think you'll be okay out here for a few minutes?"

She turned to look at him with her intense brown-eyed gaze, and her only answer was a soft, bare whisper of a bark.

"Glad to know you can speak up when you need to. I'll be right back."

He lowered the windows an inch or so, relieved the heat of the day hadn't set in yet. Still, he'd need to make it quick. When he leaned over to slip the makeshift rope leash off her neck so she wouldn't catch it on something in the truck, movement on the porch caught his eye.

Arthur Seagon, half of the husband-and-wife team who owned the bookstore and lived there too, had just stepped outside holding a small pink bucket. He was much shorter than George, and a little bit stout, but remarkably healthy looking for someone who had to be...

George had no idea how old either of the Seagons were, and his mother and grandmother had made it entirely clear there was no polite way to ask. So for a man with gray hair, a round, remarkably smooth face, and bright blue eyes, who happened to have looked exactly the same way as long as George could remember, the safest guess was over sixty.

Mr. Seagon grinned and waved as he walked down the wide steps, then his eyes widened. George guessed he'd just caught sight of the irresistible return grin from his passenger. Pink bucket abandoned beside flower beds full of exuberant bursts of red, blue, yellow, and of course, purple, Mr. Seagon stopped beside the truck with his hands clasped under his chin.

"What a *beauty*! I didn't know you had a new family member, George, congratulations! What's her name?"

George lowered the window, and barely dodged a madly wagging tail before he got a good smack in the face. Mr. Seagon giggled like a little boy as his face was showered with delicate doggie kissies.

"I don't know her name, Mr. Seagon, she just showed up this morning. I was hoping you knew where I could check to see if anyone's looking for a lost dog."

"Doesn't look like this angel is lost to me, not one little bit." Now Mr. Seagon vigorously scratched behind the dog's ears, and she turned her head from side to side so he'd get exactly the right spot. "But bring her on inside and I'll see what I can find for you."

"You sure? I don't know if she's trained for...well, you know."

Mr. Seagon pursed his lips and shook his head, as

if George had just suggested the bookstore was vivid Halloween orange and the blue sky was a most fetching shade of Day-Glo pink.

"Such silliness. I can tell by looking at her that she's a perfectly sensible girl. The compost for the flowers can wait. We'll get her a drink of water and see if she'd like a cookie or two."

George shrugged, returned the window to almost closed, got out and walked around to the sidewalk. He only realized the truck held a bit of a wet dog smell when the fresh, clean breeze of the morning after a storm filled his nose. When he opened the passenger side door, the dog didn't make any move to jump out and cause a dramatic high-speed chase down the street.

But she did stomp her front feet and whine high in her throat. An unmistakable and precious expression of *hurry, hurry, hurry!*

He held her around her chest and back legs, then lowered her to the sidewalk. She gave another of those full-body shakes before smiling up at Mr. Seagon.

"I believe she's decided we'll go inside with you," George said, twining the rope around his hand again.

Mr. Seagon clapped his hands under his chin again before starting back up the stairs.

Inside, Odds and Endings hadn't changed since George was a little boy, any more than its owners had. Row after row of every kind of book imaginable took up every inch of wall space in all the rooms he could see, expect for a few reading areas with antique chairs, tables, and lamps.

Modern hardcovers and trade paperbacks, and pretty much every variety of printed material from the last hundred years, including the smaller mass market books George and Sophie had devoured as kids. His own kids were avid readers, but more on their phones rather than in print. He'd often wondered if that was so no one would know *what* they were reading, but as long as they continued the good habit, both George and Lacy had been happy to leave them be.

The turret room at the top was where all of them first developed the reading habit, in the rounded kid-sized paradise, complete with a magical mural on the domed ceiling, lamps shaped like all kinds of whimsical creatures, and all the ancient and brand-new children's stories anyone could ask for

Today the usual comforting scent of all those books was cut through with the citrusy sharp bite of Earl Gray tea. Mr. Seagon's wife had already taken care of that part of the normal table full of refreshments for Odds and Endings customers, set up at the end of the long hallway (also lined with bookshelves).

Mr. Seagon's part of that welcome was thin, crisp,

light-as-air ginger cookies, and he was halfway down the hall to fetch them before George got himself inside and closed the door. For her part, the dog sat on the gleaming hardwood floor close beside his legs, peering around with her rapid-fire sniffing.

"Here we go," Mr. Seagon said, on his way back with a little purple napkin in each hand. George knew they'd have the stylized O and E logo on them without having to look. "Something for each of you while you wait."

George opened his mouth to ask if ginger cookies were good for dogs, but he'd never seen them shaped like cute little bones. Mr. Seagon handed the normal cookies over, then held out one of the bone cookies to the dog.

"I like to keep some of these on hand in case someone brings their best friend for a visit. Made with blueberries of all things, and oatmeal. No sugar, so they don't taste like much to a typical sweet-toothed human. But dogs love them. Ivy Gweddon's been bringing her hound dogs down here for decades, and they can't ever seem to get enough."

After a volley of sniffs and a glance up at George as if to ask permission, the dog took the cookie in her teeth with careful delicacy. She settled down full-length onto the floor to give it the attention it apparently deserved.

"Never heard of dogs liking blueberries before,"

George said, smiling. "If it's anywhere near as good as the treats you make for people, she'll eat up every crumb."

Mr. Seagon beamed and gave the other bone-shaped cookies to George.

"Well, she obviously has good taste, since she came right to you. Won't take long to see if anyone is looking for her." And he walked back down the hallway and disappeared into a door on the left.

George stepped to the side in case anyone else stopped by, then knelt when the dog looked up at him. Her tail once again brushed the floor, and she licked crumbs off her lips even as she sniffed toward his hand for more. He watched her carefully take another as he popped one of the human cookies into his own mouth and chewed, the spicy-sweet ginger taking over his senses even as it crunched away into almost nothing.

"I understand how you feel. These are like a little slice of heaven. I'll have to make sure your people know where they can get more of them for you."

He rubbed the top of her head and along her back, wishing he could take those last words back though he wasn't sure why. That reflexive chorus of reasons why he couldn't have a dog still echoed through his mind, followed by a softer echo of why the reasons didn't make sense anymore.

He wasn't home enough. Sophie often brought

one or the other of her sweet, friendly pups to work with her.

His house wasn't set up for it. None of the preparations were exactly rocket science, and Sophie had already said she'd help.

One or both of his kids might have Lacy's awful allergies, and he never, ever wanted them to feel uncomfortable or unwelcome in his home. That one was tougher, but still felt a bit creaky since both Tommy and Trina loved Sophie's dogs and cats.

The dog's obviously trusting gaze up at him brought the biggest—and most impossible to ignore —reason front and center in his mind. This wonderful girl most likely belonged to someone else.

And George didn't want to fall in love and have to watch her leave, overjoyed to be back with someone else.

"On second thought, I'll see if Mr. Seagon will set you up with a good supply before you go." He paused, scratching under her chin. "*If* you go."

They'd each finished their last treats by the time Mr. Seagon reappeared several minutes later. This time he held a couple of books instead of more cookies, but George did his best not to feel too disappointed.

"I made a few phone calls for you, George, and Carabelle is making a few more. No one has reported a missing dog of any kind, not for a long while, and I say thank goodness for that. No one had reports of one who looked like your companion there for even longer. I checked with the sheriff and everything, not just here in Lightning Gap. I think someone would have reported a delightful girl like this who was out after that storm last night, don't you?"

"Well, yeah, I think so too. That was a big, noisy one. I appreciate you checking for me. And she appreciates the treats almost as much as I do."

Mr. Seagon shrugged, but his face glowed.

"Just doing my little bit to make folks feel happy and welcome. Even more so for our four-legged visitors. That reminds me, I found your books."

George brushed his hands on his jeans and stood, shaking his head.

"I know I haven't been in for a while, and I'm overdue to spend a few hours browsing. But I didn't order any books ahead, Mr. Seagon."

"These aren't books you asked for," Mr. Seagon said, with the kind of indulgent smile someone might give to a kid afraid to take the training wheels off his bike. "They might not even be books you'd want if you did come across them on the shelf. But these are the books you need."

He held them out, and George reached for them by reflex. One was a used but well-cared-for volume about dog care for beginners, with a cartoon of a goofy grinning dog wearing professor's robes on the cover. A white dog with one floppy black ear.

The other—also with the scuffs and rounded edges showing it had been read often—featured several color photos of people of all ages with dogs or cats, and a few more unusual pets like birds, iguanas, and rats mixed in. The obvious love and affection between person and pet matched a book about animals rescuing people.

"Are these supposed to be subtle hints?" George asked, smiling.

Mr. Seagon held out both hands, and his expression was far more sincere than joking.

"I can't say I disagree with the sentiment, but times like this aren't about trying to be subtle. I'm always happy to help visitors find what they're looking for, and that's a big part of how we stay in business. We have newer pet care books in stock. But when it comes to people who live here in Lightning Gap, Carabelle and I always let Odds and Endings make the choices for us. These are *your* books, George."

George nodded, thinking he could pass them along if someone did show up to collect the dog. But this time the thought of watching her walk away got his eyes blurred with surprise tears.

He turned the books over, trying to hide it. After a couple of seconds of blinking into a smudgy haze, excerpts on the back of the rescue book slowly resolved themselves.

One about rescuing pets after children left home.

Another about pets helping with the loss of a loved one.

He tucked both under his arm and reached for his wallet.

"No, no," Mr. Seagon said. "We never allow people to pay in cases like this. Truly, the tourists and visitors do plenty to keep us going. When Odds and Endings makes it clear a special book has found a home, our greatest reward is making that happen." He paused, then winked at George. "As long as the lucky new owner *promises* to let us know how it works out."

George laughed, and he wasn't surprised to hear a low woof from the dog now standing pressed against his leg. She grinned at Mr. Seagon, then up at George.

"Well, I'd never argue with that kind of generosity. And I promise to at least let you know what happens. Deal?"

Mr. Seagon shook his outstretched hand with a firm grip.

"A bargain at twice the price. Now if you'll excuse me, I've got to help Carabelle finish the arrangements for a reading tonight. Stop by if you can, it's the first one from Ella-Jane Cole, our new author-in-residence. She's absolutely marvelous."

He bent down and rubbed the dog's ears, getting a grin and a kiss in return.

"You two have a wonderful day together," he said over his shoulder as he walked back down the hallway.

George called out "Thank you" before Mr. Seagon disappeared, then looked down at the dog. She had her head tilted again, staring after the source of the delicious treats.

"I guess Sophie was right. This was a good place to stop. Maybe we should head on down to Dr. Robinette and get you checked over, huh?" He took a deep breath and let a worried part inside relax. "Might be a good idea for you two to get to know each other."

He'd just put the books in the truck, glad he hadn't left the dog out there in the growing heat of the day, when his phone buzzed in his pocket. After the events of the morning and Mr. Seagon's calm confidence, George wasn't the least bit surprised to see a message from one of his kids, followed seconds later by one from the other.

Tommy wrote: *Dad! Aunt Sophie lasted her usual blink of an eye before she told me. Yes of COURSE you should keep the dog!*

And Trina followed up with: *How long are you*

going to make me wait for pictures of my new little sister? Rude!!!

George laughed and sat on the truck's running board at the same level as his new dog, letting her sniff his face and ears and nose before she bestowed a kissie on his chin.

"What do you think, girl? I think Mr. Seagon is right. No one would lose track of such a sweetheart without searching high and low to find you. Want to try your hand at putting up with a guy with a newly empty nest?"

She backed up two quick steps and lowered her chest to the ground, legs straight out in front and tail waving high and happy. She let out a joyful bark before charging forward and burrowing her head against George's chest.

"I'll go with yes on that one."

After a reasonable exchange of affection with his new housemate—a down payment on what he hoped would be many years to come—George got his phone back out. He opened a message to Sophie, Trina, and Tommy, and loaded up all the photos he'd taken that morning, plus a brand new cheek-to-cheek selfie.

To no one's surprise, your Aunt Sophie is way better at publicizing secrets than keeping them. In this case, she's right. Here's the new arrival. We're discussing names, but this girl has final approval. Can't wait for you all to meet her. Love, Dad.

"I'll make the first suggestion, since no one's here to argue with me yet. Since you showed up with the dawn, how about Sunny?"

This time she covered George's face with kissies before leaning her head against his shoulder and letting out one of her long, deep sighs.

"That just might be the decision made. Come on, Sunny. Let's go meet your new doc and figure out what all I need to welcome you home."

I hope you enjoyed Facing Down Extraordinary with our cast of unlikely heroes! And may we all find, or be, the heroes we need.

For more fantasy from Kari, turn the page or visit www.KariKilgore.com/Fantasy.

ALSO BY KARI KILGORE

I hope you enjoyed reading the stories in *Facing Down Extraordinary* as much as I enjoyed writing them.

Check out more of my fiction, including almost every genre, and be first to hear about release dates, Kickstarters and other fun projects, and exclusive e-book and print editions at www.KariKilgore.com.

If you'd like to catch up with Beth and Janie from *A Soggy Brush with History*, swing by www.KariKilgore.com/VoicesThroughTime.

Hugh from *Decisions in a Dangerous Situation* returns with all of his strength and courage in full bloom in my *Soul Travelers* series, beginning with *Hand Me Downs*. Find out more at www.karikilgore.com/SoulTravelers

Walt, one of the heroes from *The Best Kind of Teacher*, plays an important role several years later in my *Storms of Future Past Series*. And you might just spot Jimmy's namesake. www.karikilgore.com/StormsofFuturePast

You'll find more mystery and crime short stories, including more with Andre and his best friend Dana at www.KariKilgore.com/Mystery. And you can read the story of when Andre met Henry and Daisy Girl in *Real People Romance*.

For more stories with George from the fabulous little town

of Lightning Gap, where the magical Odds and Endings bookstore and the Seagons almost always make an appearance, visit www.KariKilgore.com/LightningGap.

For more from the Appalachian Mountains of Virginia and around the region, head over to www.KariKilgore.com/TalesFromAppalachia.

If you're looking for more fantasy tales of all kinds, check out www.KariKilgore.com/Fantasy.

Collections:

Fantastic Shorts: Volume 1

Fantastic Shorts: Volume 2

Fantastic Shorts: Volume 3

Escape into Romance

Stepping Out of Reality

Hacking Cybercrime

Investigations Beyond Belief

Passages in the Real World

Fantastic Side Trips

A Kaleidoscope of Cat Tales

A Tapestry of Holiday Tales

Aunties Among Us

Four-Legged Heroes

Anthologies *with Jason A. Adams:*

Partners in Romance

Shadows Mountain Deep

Uncommon Holidays

Partnership in Crime

Novels:

Until Death

The Dream Thief

Hand Me Downs

Protecting Her Own

The Coffee Bomb and the Corporate Spy

The Great Gold Record Heist

Novellas:

Legacy of the Land

In the Pines

Fantastic Women: A Dark Fantasy Novella Trio

DNA Never Lies

The Box of Possibilities

Murder at the Fabulous Feline Emporium

Team Building Revenge

Dispatches from the Galaxy:

Restricted Species

The Becalmed

Plurapod Pathogen

The Changes Cascade

Near Future Forward (with Jason A. Adams)

Dispatches from the Galaxy: A Space Opera Novella Trio

Dangerous Days on a Pleasure Planet

Storms of Future Past:

Dreaming the Storm

Joining the Storm

Into the Storm

Fighting the Storm

Storms of the Heart

Storms of Future Past Omnibus

Voices Through Time:

Songs in the Mountain

Secrets in the Land

Sorrows in the Earth

Walking the Ghosts

The Odd Society:

Independent by Means of Magic

Protected by Means of Magic

ABOUT KARI

Ever-inventive author Kari Kilgore's wanderlust and imagination lead her all over the world on grand adventures. Her heart and family bring her home to her native Appalachian Mountains of Virginia. From that solid base and with the help of the ever-changing lens of her imagination, she brings those adventures to life in fiction.

While Kari's certainly had her share of days that turned extraordinary, she loves writing about fictional ones. From a safe distance.

Kari writes fantasy, romance, science fiction, mystery, and contemporary fiction, and she's happiest when she surprises herself. She lives with her husband and fellow author Jason A. Adams, various house critters, and wildlife they're better off not knowing more about.

The Confidential Adventure Club

For Kari's exclusive free After The End stories and deleted scenes, discounts, early releases, adorable pet photos, Kickstarters and other fun projects, Spiral Publishing Exclusive Edition e-books and print books, and a whole lot more not available anywhere else, join us in The Club.

Hope to see you there!

www.KariKilgore.com
www.SpiralPublishing.net
www.ConfidentialAdventureClub.com

BB bookbub.com/authors/kari-kilgore

a amazon.com/author/karikilgore

g goodreads.com/karikilgore

f facebook.com/kari.kilgore.1

ADDITIONAL COPYRIGHT INFORMATION

Andre's Extra-Sensational Adventure

Copyright © 2021 by Kari A. Kilgore

All rights reserved

Published 2021 by Spiral Publishing, Ltd.

Book and cover design copyright © 2021 by Spiral Publishing, Ltd.

Cover art copyright © 2021 by chris2766 | DepositPhotos.com

Sunny with a Chance of Happiness

Copyright © 2021 by Kari A. Kilgore

All rights reserved

Published 2021 by Spiral Publishing, Ltd.

Book and cover design copyright © 2021 by Spiral Publishing, Ltd.

Cover art copyright © 2021 by hitdelight | DepositPhotos.com